ONE MORE SUNRISE

D.J. McPherson

iUniverse, Inc.
Bloomington

One More Sunrise

iUniverse books may be ordered through booksellers or by contacting:

iUniverse
1663 Liberty Drive
Bloomington, IN 47403
www.iuniverse.com
1-800-Authors (1-800-288-4677)

ISBN: 978-1-4697-7696-5 (sc)
ISBN: 978-1-4697-7697-2 (hc)
ISBN: 978-1-4697-7698-9 (e)

Library of Congress Control Number: 2012904734

Printed in the United States of America

iUniverse rev. date: 3/7/2012

ACKNOWLEDGMENTS

My first words of appreciation have to go to my wife who was the first person to see my attempts at a novel. Her words were always encouraging, and she never smirked as I came back time after time over a forty-year period and asked her to read what I had added to the story. Above all she was honest, and if there is any merit in what I have produced it is because she told me when things didn't look right.

Next I must give a blanket thank you to the hundreds of people with whom I came in contact during my twenty-nine years of naval service. Most of them are in the story in one fashion or another. Bless you all.

And finally, when the job was done except for checking details, I put a note in the Viet Nam Veterans newspaper asking for help and advice from anyone who served in Da Nang at the hospital, and anyone who served in Swift Boats. I really had no first hand knowledge of either.

I want to specifically thank former Swift Boat skipper Dave Wallace, and former Swift Boat crewmember Joe Moore. Their details about the boats and life aboard them in a wartime situation was invaluable.

I also heard from a former Air Force medic who signed his letter to me "Fat Daddy Albert Akers." Through him I learned that there was more than one hospital in Da Nang, but his recollections of the duty there closely paralleled those of retired Cdr. Anthony Arnold who served at the Naval Support Activity Hospital. It was from Cdr. Arnold's true experience, covered in an October 1966 issue of Life Magazine, that the incident of the doctors removing a live mortar round from the side of a Vietnamese solder came.

With these acknowledgments, I also wish to dedicate this book to those who served in Viet Nam -- especially those who were wounded, killed, or who never came home. May God go with them.

PREFACE

ONE MORE SUNRISE is about people affected by war; particularly two men who served their tours of duty in Viet Nam in 1967 and 1968, and those with whom their lives intertwined.

Think back over your own life and you may agree that your relationships have followed similar paths. Some friends and relatives have always been there. Some have passed away. People appeared briefly and helped you or hurt you. People you never met or even knew of took actions that changed your life.

Characters in this novel come and go in much the same way. They appear, they leave, sometimes they return, sometimes they die, much as in real life -- because this is real life for the characters in the book.

I hope you enjoy meeting those who await you.

THE LIVES OF OTHERS

When I was young, and around my imagination
There were no fences,
Each new idea
Brought excitement to my senses.
As our planet rotated and seasons changed
I could love and hope and wonder,
And my life burst forth on earth
Like God's almighty thunder.

Older I grew, and the ways of life
Quieted the thunder,
And my dreams were less of freedom,
And more of blunder.
The cruelest blow was the call to arms
That took me off to foreign lands,
To fight and bleed and hold
The lives of others in my hands.

Nurtured in churches
Where they taught God's law,
The Commandments of honor, and love
And "thou shalt not", held me in awe.
I pledged allegiance to the flag
And one nation under God.
And when my time came I was trained
And sent off with a nod.

There was no honor
In destroying lads from distant lands,
Or holding the lives
Of others in my hands.
The killer became the hero.
The one branded coward was the man of peace.
My quest became to stay alive and see
Just one more sunrise to the east.

We young men did our job
But in the doing slew our dreams.
The old men we had trusted led us
To the headwaters of Hell's streams.
Now the old men talk of the
Glory of war,
Of valor, and honor, and bravery,
On some far, distant shore.

They failed the living and
They forgot the dead.
Their deeds were false,
And they were hollow, the words they said.
Now they make new speeches
And strike up new bands
And send more young men
To hold the lives of others in their hands.

CHAPTER 1

The Pan Am flight circled over Saigon waiting to land. *The Pearl of the Orient* wasn't very impressive from the air with its sprawling, low-lying buildings and the muddy Mekong River lapping at its doorstep. Ships were offloading cargo for the war in a never-ending procedure to feed the muscle of destruction.

The landing was quick and efficient and the captain gave his usual greeting to the new guys arriving at the busiest airport in the world. The airfields in most cities handle civilian aircraft. Tan Son Nuit added fighter jets, helicopters, and military cargo planes to the mix. It was a giant anthill with a swarm of wasps thrown in to add to the confusion.

The hot, humid Vietnamese climate flooded the big jet the minute the flight attendant opened the door; it was an unpleasant welcome to a hostile land. Officers debarked first, and Jack was third off of the plane. His group was led to the terminal by a Vietnamese woman in some sort of uniform carrying a sign that said PLEASE FOLLOW ME. On the way they passed rows of aluminum boxes holding the remains of those going home early. It was a grim wakeup call for the new arrivals. Every man in line made a silent vow that he would not be one of those.

Amid the chaos of Tan Son Nuit, Jack wondered if he would ever find his way out of the place. To his surprise, he was handed a boarding pass and directed to gate 7. " Your flight to Da Nang is boarding now, Lieutenant. Your baggage is already aboard. Welcome to the war."

Jack and about 20 others were hustled aboard a C-47 cargo plane. They had to step over and around boxes of ammo, cases of beer, and medical supplies that covered every spare inch of space in order to get to their seats. He hoped his luggage made it aboard.

The old plane virtually groaned its way into the air and climbed to 5000 feet for the flight north. The pilot came on the intercom and announced that they were going to make a brief stop in some place called Cam Rahn Bay, whatever the hell that was.

After a brief stop to drop off some supplies and take on new passengers, they were on their final leg to Da Nang. They followed the coastline with broad sandy beaches that met the lush green jungle and sometimes broad fields where farmers worked their plows behind slow moving oxen. Suddenly, with no more warning than "Fasten your seat belts" the plane dropped like a rock to the earth, flaring out at the last minute before hitting the runway that went dark as they rolled out. A crew member explained the maneuver as a way to avoid ground fire when landing.

Everyone was hustled off of the plane with no ceremony or privilege for rank and directed into the terminal. Passengers were told that they could use the lavatory, but "don't dawdle or you might miss the bus and have to spend the night in a chair".

Jack took advantage of the facilities and went back to take a chair. He started to doze off when his name was called. He was led to a waiting bus and told that it made a loop of the base. "The driver knows your destination, so just listen for your name and don't worry. We'll get you home to bed." Fifteen minutes later Jack was sound asleep in his cot. His baggage was in the corner and two roommates were snoring peacefully across the room.

The next morning, Jack had a quick breakfast in the mess hall and arrived at staff headquarters early. He set his briefcase down on the steps leading to the building entrance and squinted toward the center of the compound. The sun was slightly above the horizon and directly in his eyes; he used his hand as a shield. His attention had been drawn to the ragged looking, yellow dog that shambled off the porch and wandered out to the flagpole.

There were thirteen rocks in an evenly spaced circle around the flagpole, each about the size of a basketball, and painted white in accordance with unwritten military tradition. When someone suggested that the rocks represented the original thirteen American Colonies, the petty officer in charge of maintaining the compound just shrugged. There were thirteen rocks because that's all they could find on the day the commanding officer said he wanted the place spruced up.

None of this tribute to pageantry and legend was of any interest to the shaggy dog lifting his leg on the flagpole, nor to the chattering little monkey that bounded from a nearby tree and hopped on the dog's hind quarters. One could almost hear the little creature saying giddyup as the dog trotted off to the perimeter fence to begin his morning inspection.

Each fence post was carefully checked and marked. The dog appeared satisfied with conditions as they were, but the monkey kept up a constant barrage of discontent.

After circling the entire boundary of the compound, the dog collapsed and rolled over into a satisfied heap in front of the headquarters building to begin his morning nap. The monkey jumped safely out of harm's way and scurried through the dust and disappeared into an open window.

"They do that every morning, Lieutenant. We call it the Sunrise Patrol."

Jack felt his ears get red when he realized that he had just spent several minutes engrossed in watching an old dog, with a monkey on his back, peeing on fence posts. He tried to cover with a lighthearted comment. "Are they attached to the staff?"

"Yes, sir. The dog is attached to intelligence and the monkey is our liaison with the White Mice."

"White Mice?"

"Yes, sir. The gooks' National Police."

Jack winced; terms of degradation bothered him. He wasn't even fond of most nicknames. He gave the enlisted man a hard look, but there was no malice on the man's face. "You call the local police gooks and white mice?"

"Sir, I was here for six months before I knew they had any other name."

Jack let the matter drop. "What time does the boss get in?"

The yeoman's familiar approach became more formal. He didn't know the lieutenant, but he knew that some new officer was due to report, and whoever it was would be his boss. It wouldn't be smart to get off on the wrong foot. "Commander Parks doesn't keep regular hours, sir. Most of the staff gets in about 0700. In fact, that's the Admin Officer coming now."

An amiable looking, redheaded, Lieutenant j.g. ambled up and tossed Jack what passed for a salute. With an easy drawl he asked if he had the honor of addressing Lt. John Walker, U.S. Navy.

Jack could see that this wasn't a spit and polish outfit and he fell in with the routine. "The name is Jack, and so far it's U.S. Naval Reserve, mister. You admin?"

Lt.j.g. Quincy wasn't sure how to read Jack. He seemed friendly enough, but something in his manner suggested he had a ramrod up his ass. In a distant naval orientation class there had been a remark about a good offense being worth two in the bush, or whatever. "Lt.j.g. Francis Xavier Quincy, of the St. Louis, Missouri Quincies, at your service, sir. My initials have led to the nickname Fixcue. After a couple of beers one might rearrange the pronunciation to something less desirable in mixed company. But I take no offense. And I hope you take no offense at my offering this unsolicited background information, you being our new intelligence officer and all."

Jack chuckled. "No offense taken, but a cup of coffee would do wonders for my disposition. Any inside?"

Jack picked up his briefcase and followed the officer into the Quonset hut. Other staff members began gathering around the coffee pot and Jack was introduced. The skipper and X.O. weren't in yet. He met the Supply Officer and was told that the medical officer spent most of his time at the hospital. The maintenance officer was a crusty mustang lieutenant who considered it below his dignity to report to the coffee pot area. He had spent nearly twenty years as an enlisted man before most of these young officers were out of high school. He watched them come and go with the timeless disparagement of the old veteran. If this new guy wanted to meet him, he could walk over to his desk. Jack made a point of breaking away from the gathering around him and strode over to Brick Schwartz' desk with a big smile and his hand outstretched. It worked. The maintenance officer even managed to stand up to shake hands. They both felt that protocol had been observed.

Jack was taking over as Ops officer. His predecessor had failed to follow medical procedure and resisted taking the weekly "horse pill" to ward off the malaria bug. He had developed some complications and was shipped back to the States on short notice. Without that personal contact about the job, Jack hoped that the enlisted members of the staff were up to speed so he could get to work without having to run to the X.O. for everything. He did know for sure that the big yellow dog was in his department. He would have to check on the monkey.

Introductions over, everyone fell into the daily routine. Fixcue showed Jack to his desk near the back door of the Quonset hut. While he was cleaning out the drawers and putting the desktop in order, Jack wondered if he had made a mistake volunteering for Viet Nam. He started navy life with intentions of doing the three years of service that his naval reserve officer candidate school training obligated him to. Then he would get out and find a good job. Despite the rigors of destroyer life, he enjoyed his first tour of duty. The travel was interesting. The sea duty was exciting, and for the first time in his life he had more money than he needed. When his tour was coming to an end, his detail officer in Washington, D.C. offered him a split tour of duty on a cruiser followed by a chance at staff duty in Washington, or possibly even the Naval War College. He would have to obligate for three more years. It was a good opportunity for a reserve officer, especially if he decided later to apply for a regular commission. It was too good to pass up.

While he was growing up, Jack's family lived close to the poverty line, partially because of the circumstances of poorly educated parents and mostly because his father drank up more of his paycheck than he contributed to the family. His mother worked hard as a part time waitress to keep the family together, but her meager earnings didn't contribute much beyond the basic necessities. She loved her husband, in spite of his failings, and she loved her children; that's why she kept trying. Jack worked regularly while he was in high school at the expense of never being able to participate in the sports that he loved. He gave his mother money whenever he could. She always tried to refuse his offerings telling him to take care of himself and buy some nice clothes for school. In the end she took the money because she needed it. She didn't expect anything from him; her goal in life was to see her children free of the existence she had to bear. Jack's older brother had taken his mother's advice and left home when he was sixteen years old. To this day Jack had no idea where his older brother was.

Jack's mother lived to see him graduate from high school. It was the proudest moment of her life. His father had planned to come to his graduation, but he stopped on the way to fortify himself at Kesler's Bar. He never made it to the ceremony. It was a blessing to Jack because he lived in fear of his father showing up drunk and embarrassing him the way he had so many other times. Jack's mother died that summer after graduation. She had been living with a painful breast cancer that she allowed to get out of control before going to the clinic for help. She knew that it would cost money and she had none. By the time she finally sought help it was too late. She endured two operations. The doctors were planning other treatments, but in her heart she felt she couldn't go on. It didn't have to be that way. With the additional treatment she could have continued her life for several years; perhaps it was that possibility that made her just give up.

Jack moved away from home right after the funeral. His father lost the house to the bank within a year after his wife died. Jack found a room to rent and worked wherever he could. He clerked at the drug store days, took tickets at the theatre evenings, and did odd jobs on the weekends. He made enough to pay his rent and other bills, but he wasn't able to save anything. He had a vague idea about going to college, but all he really knew about college was that it would cost more money than he had. His boss at the drug store appreciated Jack's hard work. One day he introduced him to Max Welt, business secretary at the local laborers' union. He didn't want to lose a good employee at the drug store, but he knew that Jack could make twice the money he was making on all his jobs if he got hired on through the union. It was a good opportunity and Jack told the union boss that he would do his best if he would just give him a chance.

Max took Jack under his wing and started him in the direction that was to give meaning to his life. He put him on the best jobs and coaxed the foremen to throw some overtime his way. Jack responded by being the best worker on every job he was sent to. Around the union hall there were the same faces every morning. Workers who would go out on a job and last only a day or two before quitting for some imagined reason of mistreatment. Some didn't even make it to the noon whistle. Jack was never one of those. In fact, some of the old timers on the jobs told him to slow down and pace himself; he was making the rest of them look bad by comparison. But he didn't slow down and the foremen noticed him. He moved into better jobs with better pay and by the end of the year Jack had saved two hundred dollars. The following summer he had enough of a nest egg to start college. Max Welt couldn't have been happier if Jack were his own son. Like the drugstore owner, Max didn't want to lose a good worker, but he knew that his young protege was destined for bigger things.

Jack's first choice was the University of San Francisco, a Catholic Jesuit school with a great basketball team. But it was a private school and tuition was high. At the state college, tuition and books were affordable and a dorm with kitchen privileges was available at rock bottom prices. There were jobs available through the school employment office, and he could work summers on the union jobs. If he stuck with what he could afford he could make it through college.

When he went to San Francisco State College to apply for entrance, he wasn't sure what subject to major in. College prep wasn't even a topic of conversation in his family, and no one had ever taken the time to discuss the matter with him. His counselor at high school judged him by his family and wrote him off as a college prospect. His high school background was weak in math and science; in fact, academically, he didn't have much at all going for him. It was luck, not planning, that he managed to squeak by with enough prerequisites to be admitted to college. But there was more to education than what was covered in the classrooms. While he was still in grammar school he had read an article in the newspaper about Harry Truman, the new President of the United States. The article said that Truman wasn't much of a student at school, but that he was self-educated through a habit of reading. There was a list of books that Mr. Truman recommended. Among them Gibbon's *Decline and Fall of the Roman Empire*. The title made it sound like a rip- roaring adventure tale and Jack went to the library to check it out. The book came in two volumes and he could barely carry them. The librarian knew that he wouldn't make it through the long, dry passages, but she encouraged him to try. Just checking out such classical literature was a step in the right direction, she thought. His first encounter with Gibbon's tale ended much as the Roman Empire had. It sort of petered out.   Throughout his high school years he kept at the great "Decline", checking it out from the library from time to time, and eventually he felt that he had read the whole story. Time and again he found passages that inspired him or made him think. It was a worthwhile endeavor. He enjoyed reading and developed the habit of trying to read a new book every month. It was a discipline that educated him in a wide variety of subjects that didn't show up on his high school transcript. He had done fairly well in the few English classes he had taken and he enjoyed history, but his true education, his logic, and his ability to sort out problems and correct them came from his outside reading.

The guys hanging around the union hall all seemed to agree that politicians led a pretty good life so Jack decided on Political Science as a major. Political Science had a nice ring to it and there was the added advantage that with a few extra credits he might be able to earn a teaching credential to fall back on.

He eventually made it through college without particular distinction. At the midway point he had to drop out and work full time, which set him back a semester, but he kept at it to graduation. To supplement his income while going to college he had joined the naval reserve as a seaman recruit. Once a week he went to meetings at Treasure Island and once a year he spent two weeks in training. He earned a full day's pay for each two-hour meeting and he earned full pay and allowances on the two week cruises. The first year he spent his two weeks at boot camp; summers after that he reported to a ship for on-the-job training at sea.

One night, at a reserve meeting, the executive officer gathered everyone who was going to college in the coffee lounge and explained that the navy had an officer training program for members of the enlisted reserve. Jack remembered being aboard ship and peeking into the officers' quarters during his two week cruises. An impression that really stuck with him was the day he was standing in the chow line waiting to go down the ladder into the mess hall. The line passed the officers' ward room where lunch was also about to be served. There was a white linen tablecloth on the dining table and cloth napkins and porcelain plates and silver service. The mess stewards were preparing to serve the meal. After that glimpse, Jack descended the ladder into the enlisted mess and took a tin tray off the rack and passed through the chow line. He picked up his silverware and a paper napkin at the end of the line and found a place to sit at a crowded mess table. He had no concept of the requirements, or the training, or the responsibilities of being an officer, but he swore then and there that if he ever had a chance to get off the mess decks he would do it. And now the chance was presenting itself. The exec was droning on about naval tradition and heroic officers that had gone before. He talked about opportunities and training and navy life. But he didn't need to sell Jack. The white tablecloth in the officers' wardroom was beckoning to him.

Jack compiled a good record in his early naval career. The War College billet didn't come through, but the consensus among his superiors at the Pentagon on his staff tour was that if he spent a tour in Viet Nam he could count on the War College when he came home. So, Jack volunteered and here he was. His wife, Sally, had listened to his reasoning when he told her what he was planning and she backed his decision, although Jack sensed some hesitation in her manner. They had gotten married in San Diego while he was stationed aboard the cruiser. The first baby arrived a month before his orders to Washington came. Just before he got on the plane to come to Viet Nam Sally told him that she had a feeling another child was on the way, but she wasn't sure yet. It had been a big decision to leave for a war that was becoming unpopular even in some military circles, but he had decided to apply for a regular commission and this was a logical career move. He questioned his decision every day because of how it would affect his family. He would make it up to them somehow.

Jack was leaning back in his chair lightly drumming his knee with the eraser of a pencil when he heard a staccato clicking coming toward him. He looked up to see the very precise form of the staff executive officer. Everyone in Viet Nam wore camouflage fatigues except the X.O. He had on starched work khakis, regulation cap, and the most brightly shined shoes in Asia. Jack got a good look at the shoes when the X.O. put his foot up on the desk and started cleaning the dust from the polished leather. He was a pinched faced man, small in stature, but perfect in every detail of his being. Precisely fitting uniform, neatly trimmed moustache, rimless glasses, but to some surprise he had a soft, delicate, handshake.

"Pleasure to meet you, Walker. Come into my office as soon as you get settled." No banter, no small talk. All business this one, thought Jack.

"Yes, sir. I can join you at your convenience, sir. Should I come in now or give you a few minutes to start the day?"

"I just told you as soon as you get settled. Do I have to spell it out plainer than that?" The X.O. marched into his office and slammed the door.

Oh, shit, thought Jack, another one of those. The navy was filled with one-upsman-shippers who had to establish authority over everyone junior to them with sarcastic and belittling remarks; more often with questions delivered in an accusing tone. A favorite of the first X.O. that Jack had served under aboard the destroyer was to ensure that no incoming radio traffic was routed to anyone before he saw it. Then he would waylay some unsuspecting junior officer, ask him if he had seen the latest weather report, and then raise hell because the poor bastard hadn't read an obscure incoming message that he probably wasn't even on routing for. Meal times were the worst. When they were at sea, the commanding officer often stayed on the bridge and missed meals in the wardroom. That martinet of an exec took his place at the head of the table and spent the entire dining time tossing out impossible questions and following up with sarcastic accusations of incompetence. Even worse, the man considered himself an epicure. The wardroom food was always sub-standard in his opinion and the lack of a decent bottle of wine with dinner was unacceptable. He managed to denigrate the manners of at least one officer at every meal. And worst of all, he flouted naval tradition for his own personal gratification. It was standard procedure in a small wardroom for the mess stewards to place the "buck", a small statue or object, at a different seat each night so that everyone would have an equal chance of being served first. The X.O. insisted that he be served first in all cases and then the stewards could go next to the officer with the buck. Thus, he assured himself of the choicest cut of meat or whatever was being served. Then he would make a great exhibition of making his selection. He had the infuriating habit of wielding the serving utensils with one hand. It took him far longer than necessary to get the food to his plate because he wasn't very adept, and he also had to look under each piece of meat as he was making his choice. All the officers wondered if he expected to find a bug in the food or something. Through all this the poor mess steward was bent over holding the serving tray and trying not to dump the whole thing in the exec's lap. It was touch and go when a heavy sea was running. Jack suffered badly under the man and swore that if he ever ran into another one of those sons-of-bitches he would stand his ground at the first meeting and refuse to be bullied.

So here goes, Jack muttered to himself. He strode up to the XO's door and stood for a moment contemplating the mahogany nameplate with the gold lettering: Archer M. Hilgo, Lieutenant Commander, USN, Executive Officer. Jack rapped sharply, twice, and walked in without waiting for a reply. He stood at the desk in a parade rest stance and said "You weren't specific about why you wanted to see me, sir. Shall I get my service record, or is there anything else I should have brought along?"

The X.O. missed only half a beat before he started in on Jack. "I don't see your note pad or pencil, lieutenant. When you report to me, come prepared to deliver information and take notes. I've already reviewed your record. No need to go over that again." He threw a pad and pencil across the desk and motioned Jack to a chair. Hilgo asked a few personal questions about Jack's family, his last assignment, and what duties he had experience in. Indeed, small talk was not his forte.

Before Jack could answer the last question the X.O. had wearied of the obligatory introductory banter and was rattling off assignments, boat numbers, names, meeting dates, and in all, over a dozen specifics that he expected taken care of before noon.

This is it, thought Jack. "Sir, I just got off the plane from Tan Son Nuit two hours ago. I've been travelling for the last 48 hours without a decent night's sleep. I haven't unpacked my bags except to get my shaving kit out, and I just found my desk five minutes ago. Unless you expect us to be under attack before the sun goes down, I'd sure as hell appreciate at least one day to get organized before you lay a full work schedule on me."

When the X.O. rose slowly to his feet Jack followed his lead and stood at attention facing him across the desk with a steady, uncompromising gaze. "Very well, lieutenant. If you haven't been getting your normal rest lately, by all means go take a nap. I'll find someone to cover your duties for you. Report back to me when you feel you can keep up."

Jack spread his heels slightly apart and snapped back to attention with a loud click and in an exaggerated voice almost shouted "Yes, sir. Thank you, sir." Then he did a smart about face and marched out of the office closing the door with a solid thump. He called to the yeoman over his shoulder that he was going over to take a nap and that he would be back after lunch. The only sound in the Quonset hut as he strode out the front door was the measured clapping of the staff maintenance officer who was delighted to see that the new Ops officer had a solid set of balls.

CHAPTER 2

About the same time when Lt. Jack Walker was settling into his operations duties with the squadron, a young marine named Geoffrey Dunlay was starting a leave period following advanced infantry training at Camp Pendleton, California. His parents picked him up at the Oakland Airport. It was a joyous family reunion. His brother and sister were there and the family stopped at Rossburg's best restaurant for dinner on the way home. Much to celebrate Geoffrey's visit home, but also to show off their favorite marine to the town. Phil Dunlay, was bursting with a father's pride. He made a point of waving to people he knew and pointing to the handsome young guest of honor at his table.

People stopped by the table and said hello. One of them was the high school football coach. "You look as fit as ever, young fellow. How about stopping by our spring workout tomorrow and saying a few words to the team. You're kind of legend with the young players."

"Thanks, coach. I wasn't sure you'd want me hanging around after the problems I had."

There was an awkward silence at the table as thoughts went back to the young marine's senior year in high school. Two weeks before graduation Geoffrey, or Jeff, as he was known, had spent a night in jail after leading the local police on a wild chase through the back roads and over some fire trails. The gang had met at the lake for a pre-graduation beer bust and Jeff was one of the gang. It was a great party among friends who had known each other most of their lives. When it finally ended late in the night the beer keg was empty and Jeff had drunk more than his share. The sheriff's car was coming down the road just as Jeff roared out onto the highway. He tried to leave the red light and siren behind by going off road, but he ended up on a dead end dirt trail and there was no escape when the police pulled up behind him. Even if he had gotten away it would have been a shortlived evasion. Rossburg was in a rural area and the police knew who everyone was and who drove which truck.

"How do you plead, Geoffrey?" the judge asked. Judge Banes was the epitome of authority. A shock of white hair just bordering on the untamed side, and a square, handsome face bordering on the flushed, reddish side rose above the black judicial robe. All of this menace peered down on Jeff who was feeling very alone and weak in the hot, stuffy courtroom.

His reply was barely audible. "Guilty, ...sir?"

The judge had dealt with many of the young people in town. He knew Jeff, but this wasn't a social visit. This was courtroom justice. Apprehension, trial, decision and punishment. Swift and sure. He had heard all the stories and the excuses. He had listened to the promises of the parents who had tried, the threats of the parents who had failed, and the sobs of the parents who hadn't even realized that their children were capable of getting into trouble, much less actually in trouble. "You admit to drinking and driving recklessly?"

"I only had a couple of beers, sir."

"Then I'll have to assume that it only takes a couple of beers to ruin your judgment and make you act like a jackass."

"Yes, sir."

"Weren't you up before me last year for taking part in that riot at the drive in?"

"It wasn't exactly a riot." He wanted to say more, but this wasn't a fight he could win. There had been a fight at the drive-in when words were exchanged between students from Port Chicago and Rossburg after a football game. Jeff hadn't even been in the fight, but when the police arrived he was in the middle of the crowd that had formed around a few boys who were scuffling. Several people had come to court after that incident and spoke in Jeff's behalf.

Jeff broke the school rushing record that year and was named All State, Second Team Half Back. At that trial his football coach had spoken at some length about his leadership qualities, his cool-headed approach to difficult situations, and he had told the judge that if there was a fight, Jeff would more likely be the one trying to break it up. His reputation around Rossberg High following the few fights that he did have was that Jeff Dunlay was the wrong guy to pick on.

Following the coach, Jeff's former scoutmaster got up to talk. He had told how the young man had become an eagle scout the year before, and about Jeff's willingness to work with the younger boys. On troop camp-outs Jeff was one of the most popular kids in the troop because he knew how to cook; everyone wanted to share his campfire.

One of Jeff's teachers came to court and had testified that Jeff had been elected the junior class president. His grades were average, and he had never received a grade below a "C". He was a hard working student.

Judge Banes rarely saw the kind of support that Jeff had. Some teenagers were lucky to have their parents show up in court with them. It was because of that support that he excused Jeff after the drive-in incident. He had only brought the matter up during this trial to stall for time. He knew all about Jeff, how he earned his own spending money with a small attic and cellar cleaning and trash hauling business he started with a fifty-dollar loan from his father. The fifty dollars bought half interest in the jalopy pick up truck; the other half was owned by Bill Banes who shared most of Jeff's fortunes, whether good or ill. It was a stroke of luck that Bill wasn't with Jeff on the night of the chase. If he had been, Judge Banes would have had to recuse himself from the case. Better the devil you know than some out of town judge with no respect for local football rushing records.

Judge Banes knew that Jeff was an energetic teen-ager, a handsome young fellow and a gifted athlete popular with everyone.

But popular or not, this was serious business and the facts were leading to a harsh decision. There was a stirring in the court and Judge Banes realized that he had allowed himself to daydream just a bit too long.

"May I speak, sir?" The voice was commanding. Standing at stiff attention, his hat under his left arm and his chest a glittering display of ribbons and stars, was Gunnery Sergeant Emil Kline, United States Marine Corps. The sergeant introduced himself with such authority that Judge Banes almost stood up to salute. He was delighted with the interruption because he wasn't ready to impose a sentence just yet.

"Are you interested in this case, Sergeant?"

A touch of a smile curled the sergeant's lips, but his eyes were hard. It was easy to understand the terror an enemy -- or a marine recruit -- would experience facing him. He ignored Jeff and his father and spoke directly to the judge. "Sir, I have spent two months of my time and a considerable amount of the government's money preparing to enlist Geoffrey Dunlay in the Corps. I don't condone breaking the law, but on the other hand, we can't enlist a man with a police record. The offense is serious, but if Your Honor will see fit to release young Dunlay to me for the next two weeks until he graduates, his father willing of course, I'll guarantee that he will be in no more trouble until he leaves town for training. That will be the day after graduation."

The cavalry to the rescue, the judge thought to himself. He stroked his chin and gave every appearance of deep thought and consideration. He did such a good job of acting that he fooled Phil Dunlay who had come to court with his son. Finally he spoke.

"Mr Dunlay," the judge addressed Jeff's father "what do you have to say to the sergeant's proposal?" And he thought to himself: If you say anything but "yes", I'll fine you for stupidity.

"Your Honor, I've given my consent for Jeff to join up. In a way I feel he has already left home. If you are willing to accept the sergeant's proposal, I'll go along."

It turned out to be a fairly simple solution to what could have been a real can of worms. Judge Banes had thought of recusing himself because of his son's close relationship, but neither side had expressed any objection to his hearing the case and he felt that he could serve justice and do the right thing. Up until the sergeant's intervention, he was feeling badly squeezed and wished he had let some other judge handle this matter.

"Very well. Geoffrey Dunlay, from here on you are in the hands of the United States Marine Corps. This case will be held open until you report for training. If you can stay out of trouble for the next two weeks, I'll drop the charges. Do you have anything to say?"

What the hell, thought Jeff. Is there a choice? "No, sir."

The gavel banged and Jeff Dunlay was a marine. Now, nearly a year later, the boyhood missteps that could have led him down a very different path were all but forgotten by his former coach and most of the town.

The awkwardness melted away at the dinner table as the coach clapped Jeff on the back and said, "Be at the field at 3:30 tomorrow if you can. Wear your uniform." Everyone at the table started talking at once. It was great having the local hero back in the fold.

The next day, Jeff showed up at the practice field on the dot of 3:30. The coach called a halt to the drills and gathered everyone around Jeff to introduce him. There were a few players that had been on the team when Jeff played, but to most of them he was a stranger. Contrary to the coach's thinking, some in the group had never heard of Jeff Dunlay. The young marine shook hands with a few of the players and told them all how he hoped they were going to have a big year next season. Jeff could see that there wasn't much interest in his presence. The coach had given him a big build up and led what turned out to be a smattering of applause during the introduction. A couple of boys started tossing a ball back and forth and there was mumbling in the back row. Jeff broke it off quickly. "Thanks for letting me come by, coach. Good luck next season." He waved as he walked quickly off the field. Spring practice was back in full swing before he reached the edge of the playing area. He stopped for a moment and looked back. There was a pang of regret as he realized that he was no longer a part of that team. He had been their leader a short time ago, now he was just another interfering adult screwing up spring practice.

Back at home, Jeff shocked his mother by taking one of his father's beers out of the refrigerator and sitting down at the kitchen table and drinking it without so much as saying please. "When did you start drinking, Geoffrey?"

"It's just a beer, mom." He told his mother about the experience at the field. He couldn't quite explain how he felt, but his mother knew what was happening.

"You're growing up, Jeff. Sometimes when you try to go back it hurts a little. High school boys can be difficult." Jeff's mother went on trying to explain to her son what she knew about young boys. "Before the day is over the word will be all over town that Jeff Dunlay visited football practice. The boys who were on the team when you played will all be telling stories about how well they knew you and what good buddies you all were. You wait and see. Next time you go downtown kids will be asking for your autograph."

It wasn't as exciting as his mother had predicted, but the former football hero turned marine did get more attention than he expected during his ten day leave that went by so quickly. Jeff learned one of life's lessons. Being a hero only counts while you're doing heroic things. The people who made you a hero yesterday probably won't remember you now that you aren't doing anything for their benefit. Don't count on the past to get you through the future.

★ ★ ★

Those days on the football field, and his visit home, were distant memories now, separated by the months Jeff had been in Viet Nam. He had been assigned to a rifle company and was in and out of the bush from the first week he reported for duty. This was a different world from the one he left behind in the States. A gentle breeze rustled the grass and brought him back to reality. Back to the hot humid air, the flying bugs, the smell of night soil from the direction of the hamlet a few hundred yards away. He watched casually as a seven-inch centipede came out of the grass and worked its way nearer to him. It was an arrogant creature with the confidence to go wherever it pleased. Jeff watched it crawl over his foot and back into the grass as he remembered Mrs. Lasky's admonishment to the biology class as she explained anthropoids: "Don't step on them. They may seem ugly to us, but to another centipede they are beautiful."

The village was quiet. There were no kids running around, none of the usual activity. Those were bad signs. The lieutenant had put Jeff out on the right flank with Kiley and Smolen. Just the day before the lieutenant had announced Jeff's promotion to corporal in front of the platoon. He was a veteran of six months in Viet Nam, a lifetime of experience. Some people don't make it past the first day. He had proven himself. He was a fighter and a natural leader, and he had a way of quietly taking charge when things needed to be done.

Now he was leading a small detachment and lives depended on him. He had a feeling about the coming operation. Jeff was going to say something when the lieutenant put out the word about how they were deploying for the day's business, but privates and corporals don't comment on an officer's order. That's what gunnery sergeants exist for. The "gunny" helps the second lieutenant stay alive long enough to make first lieutenant. His other job is to plant a size 12 shoe up the ass of any Grunt dumb enough to think he knows more than the officers.

Jeff and his men watched the village. He could see the platoon moving forward. The lieutenant was in the lead. He walked slowly; if he was worried about anything it didn't show. An old man sat at the far end of the hamlet smoking a pipe. Jeff could make out the wisps of hair on his long chin whiskers. Like a caricature on a *Visit the Orient* travel poster. Further to the right, in the field, another man struggled with a crude plow behind a water buffalo. A little river of perspiration ran down Jeff's slightly crooked nose. It followed almost exactly the broken cartilage that was the only imperfect feature on his face. Right now it was hard to see the face under the dust and grime from two days in the field. The dark red, almost bronze colored, hair faded into the natural camouflage.

The last time Jeff saw the lieutenant was when he disappeared behind one of the grass huts. An instant later the area exploded in a cloud of fire and dirt. The men nearing the village froze. Someone, probably the lieutenant, had stepped on a land mine and it triggered several others. For a fraction of a moment the world stopped turning. No one moved; the old man was smoking his pipe; the water buffalo was standing quietly and the man with the plow was a statue. Dust hung in the air with death and silence. Any place a man stepped now could be onto a mine. The village had been set up as an ambush. It was only a matter of seconds and then the whole area erupted again. This time it was mortars. No use worrying about the mines. The platoon scattered. It was a hell of a spot and there was no way to tell where the mortars were coming from. Charlie had the hamlet zeroed in. Charlie was the Viet Cong guerilla. V.C. Victor Charlie in the military phonetic alphabet.

"Let's go! Move!" Jeff was up and running with Kiley and Smolen on his heels. His instincts led them to a spot about a hundred yards from where they had started. They could hear the "woomph" of the mortar rounds leaving the tube.

Jeff spread out his tiny force and he moved forward with his M-79 grenade launcher loaded and ready. He could see three mortars working about a hundred and fifty yards ahead. Jeff began firing and reloading as fast as he could; his flankers poured in rounds from their M-16s as they rushed the mortars. Kiley went down. At first Jeff thought Kiley had tripped and fallen; but he was dead, a bullet between his eyes and the back of his head blown out. "Keep moving, Mike. It's our only chance," Jeff ordered.

Then Smolen went down screaming and holding his left hip. He struggled back up on one knee and called Jeff's name and a volley of shots ripped into him. Jeff was alone. He fired his last grenade and swung his M-16 rifle into a firing arc before the discarded grenade launcher hit the ground. What had been three mortar crews became an army. Jeff found himself facing about fifteen V.C. in their black pajama uniforms. He was in the open running toward them. Once again the world went into slow motion. He could see the faces of the enemy as they raised their weapons and fired at him. They were individuals. Mostly young, some angry, some frightened, some calmly taking aim and planning to kill him.

There was a searing pain as a punji stake went through Jeff's boot. It was just a sharp piece of bamboo sticking up from a hole, but it was a hell of an effective way to stop a man. Jeff thought he felt the stake go all the way to his heart; then something slammed into his chest and knocked him unconscious.

★ ★ ★

A week later in the suburbs, about six thousand miles to the east, pot roast, potatoes, string beans and jello had been on the evening menu. Two parents and two teenagers were in the living room of the modest house on the street lined with modest houses. President Lyndon Johnson was on the television telling the American people that 1967 was the year of victory in Viet Nam. The enemy was on the edge of defeat. Not everyone on the street believed that the bloody war six thousand miles to the west was going to end. Not with the continued Draft, the increasing troop buildup, and the carnage dominating the evening TV news.

"He's your brother, Lester. Doesn't that mean anything to you?"

"Sure it does, but he has no business in Viet Nam." Lester stood his ground. His father was a sedentary man. The raging and roaring, and wild arm movements had a comical effect coming from the paunchy, bald headed little fellow.

"He has more business in Viet Nam than you have saying he got what was coming to him. He's you brother. You're both my sons."

"What the hell, Dad, tell me the truth. If the pill had been available seventeen years ago would I be here now?"

"Dammit, Lester, that's no way to talk."

Mrs. Dunlay interrupted. She was a quiet woman with vestiges of youthful beauty lurking around her eyes and mouth; but these days sorrow dominated. She and her husband had stood in this same room just a week before while the Navy Chaplain and the Marine Lieutenant told them that their elder son was missing in action and possibly captured by the enemy in Viet Nam.

"Can't you two ever talk to each other? Especially at a time like this…" Her words trailed off and her shoulders heaved as she sank into an easy chair, sobbing.

Jeff had left for recruit training the day after graduation from high school. And now, a year later, Jeff Dunlay was a statistic. One of those vague statistics that burn in a parent's heart. Not dead. Not wounded. Not anything. Just missing. What does that mean? Blown into so many pieces that he couldn't be found? Lying in a ditch wounded and helpless, unable to call out for help? Being dragged along at the end of a rope by an enemy soldier through some nameless jungle?

Phil Dunlay looked at his younger son, Les, and wanted to hit him. How could a child he raised stand there and as much as say that his brother deserved what happened to him. What brought this on? The two boys had gotten along well. Having a sister in the middle as a buffer helped. But there was nothing to show this side of Les. Phil didn't understand.

One night, just before Jeff left for Viet Nam, he and Les had sat up until early in the morning talking about all the things young men could chew on for hours. The war was mentioned, but it wasn't their main topic of conversation. Mostly they talked about the future and what they planned to do with their lives. Jeff's life centered on sports. Beyond that he didn't give it much thought. College maybe, but nothing specific. He had no burning career goal. Les, on the other hand, had given his future a good deal of thought. He leaned heavily toward science. Medical school perhaps, although law and politics were considerations. The interesting thing was that both accepted the other without question.

Otherwise the brothers were nothing alike. Jeff was outgoing, physical, and athletic. He was the protector and he had always looked out for his little brother. Les had none of the drive and dash of his older brother, but in many ways he was more mature. His tutoring had helped Jeff through his senior year math classes. He read voraciously, loved school, studied hard, and had a consuming interest in world affairs. He read the paper every day. He could talk about business trends, world trade, emerging nations, the environment, and although it wasn't his primary interest, he had a good grasp of sports statistics. His teachers had a hard time keeping him occupied in class. He seemed to already know most of what they were teaching.

Shortly after Jeff left for recruit training, and summer vacation had started, Les dropped a bombshell on the family. He asked his parents to listen to a speech he had prepared for delivery at a rally being held in San Francisco over the weekend. His father was interested at first. He knew his son was a member of several clubs at school and he assumed that this was a summer carry over of some group or other.

"Let's have it, Les." Phil motioned to his wife and daughter, with a wink, to have a seat. "Sit down, girls. Let's hear what our young orator has to say for himself."

"P E A C E" boomed young Les. "Why must the brotherhood of man forever live with war and hate? Why must we allow the wealthy industrialists to force young men to fight and die for trumped up causes? There is no need for the cream of American youth to be killing and dying in Viet Nam. We could all be living in peace..."

The elder Dunlay listened. He waited for the punch line because this was surely some kind of joke.

"...rather than your sons and brothers fighting a war thousands of miles from home. Young men must resist. Anyone who goes to war to fight for the politicians and the wealthy are not only fools, they are betraying the ideals of their country."

Anita Dunlay thought about her son in training for a far off war and started to shift uneasily in her chair. Her hand reached out and she touched her husband's arm.

Phil Dunlay realized that this was no joke. In his mind it was Commie propaganda pure and simple. "Just a minute, Les. What kind of a rally are you going to attend this week-end?" Phil tried to control his voice, but this was off the deep end. No patriotic boy should harbor these thoughts. This wasn't how Americans talked when their troops were at war. His baldhead started to turn red. Les recognized the signs.

"Forget it, Dad. I knew you wouldn't listen."

"Dammit. Who's going to this rally?"

"Just a bunch of people. Everyone gets up and says whatever he wants. No one makes a big deal out of it. It's sort of a public speaking group."

"Does this group have a name?"

"No. They don't believe in titles."

"Where do they come from, these public speakers without titles?"

"All over. You wouldn't understand."

"I understand enough to know that you aren't going to leave this house this week-end or any other week-end until you get these goofy ideas out of your head."

"May I leave now?" Jeff said with a sigh.

"Get to your room." Phil Dunlay was really shaken; his own son was patronizing him. Not yet sixteen years old and he knows the world's troubles, thought Phil. His whole head turned the color of an overripe tomato. "Get to your room." he screamed.

It had never been like this with Jeff; he understood Jeff. He couldn't deal with Les. He never knew what the boy was thinking. Phil had a vagrant thought that he hadn't really listened to Les or tried to find out what he was thinking. But what the hell, thought Phil, the kid should be thinking about girls or something, not trying to save the world from a park bench. Didn't he realize that his own brother was one of the people he was denouncing?

And now, with his brother missing in action for over a week, Les was still carrying on with his nitwit ideas. Phil threw up his arms and walked out of the room leaving his wife crying and his son smirking. His daughter Susie started after him then stopped and went to her mother who waved her away. She plopped down on the sofa and stared after her younger brother as he headed toward the kitchen for seconds on dessert.

"What's happening?" thought Phil. The family was in turmoil. Jeff was missing in action in a war on the other side of the globe, Les was acting out some strange, teen-aged fantasy that Phil couldn't understand, and his wife Anita was sinking into a terrible depression. He hadn't noticed the tear running down Susan's cheek to the corner of her mouth.

CHAPTER 3

Out in the South China Sea, off the coast of Viet Nam, the Swift Boat eased through the dark waters. PCF, Patrol Craft Fast was the boat's official designation. It was 50 feet of 3/8" aluminum with two big diesel engines, a twin .50 caliber machine gun forward and a single .50 aft often mounted over an 81 mm mortar. The boats were built from the keel up to work in the shallow waters near the coast and up the many rivers that flowed out of Viet Nam. Out in the ocean waters it was often a rough ride and crew members were used to bangs and bruises from being thrown around when the weather acted up.

Tonight, the dark sea was like a lake. Hardly even a breeze to ruffle the waters. Lieutenant Jack Walker came up on deck from the small, cramped galley, crew quarters, and all purpose living area aft of the pilot house. Jack sometimes came out on patrols with his boats although his job was back at the base coordinating patrol activities. The pencil got heavy and the piles of paper were like a prison to him. He missed the freedom of being at sea. Joining a patrol also gave him a chance to get to know the boat crews a bit better. They were a tight knit group and Jack assumed, probably correctly, suspicious of the staff pukes that sent them off on their various missions.

It didn't hurt anything to take a ride once in a while. The C.O. didn't mind, even when he was sober. Jack still clashed with the X.O., but ever since that first day many months ago when Jack walked out of the office to take a nap there was a grudging truce between the two. Jack always thought of Archer Hilgo as a four star pain in the ass, but he had to admit that the qualities he despised in the man were the ones that made him an outstanding officer. He was honest, he knew his job, and he was consistent. You knew where you stood with Hilgo, even if you sometimes felt like you were standing in six feet of pig dung.

The C.O. was on a twilight tour, his last before retiring. The twilight tour was often a soft job that rounded out the final months of an officer's career so that he could wind down and prepare for civilian life. But Cdr. Milton Parks had taken one drink too many and pissed off the wrong admiral, or more precisely, the wrong admiral's wife shortly before becoming eligible for retirement. It was a long story, the crux being a drunken brawl, a badly stained oriental rug, and a "Mrs. Admiral" so badly irked about the ruination of her annual spring party that she wanted Cdr. Parks hung from the Washington Monument as a warning to all who might throw up on her precious rug. It wasn't Milton Parks' only transgression in Washington, D.C.'s military society, but it was his last one. The best the admiral could do was have Parks shipped to Viet Nam to complete his career and make it to retirement. No matter how badly an officer screwed up, his fellow officers tried to protect his retirement. And in Viet Nam the luck of Cdr. Parks held up in the essence of LCDR Archer Hilgo. Hilgo carried his C.O., protected him, served as his alter ego, and sobered him up when the occasion demanded. When the big brass came up from Saigon, Cdr. Parks was always at his desk. Archer Hilgo's method was classic. He knew that Parks loved to play bridge. He would get him into a bridge game the night before some activity required his sobriety. Bridge got his mind off the liquor and if they could keep the game going long enough, the Commander was too tired to get drunk after the game was over. All that was left was to be sure to catch him in the morning before he had a chance to start on the Bloody Marys.

The bridge games were one more thing that Jack was in trouble with Hilgo about. Poker was Jack's game. He had never had time to learn the game of bridge. While his college friends were sitting around the cafeteria every afternoon learning the fine points of the game, Jack was working, trying to keep ahead of his bills. He tried to fake it when he was invited to play the first and last time the X.O. asked him to sit in. The night was a disaster because Jack had scant knowledge and his bidding was pathetic. And to make matters worse, he was a regular at Cdr. Parks' poker games. The C.O. loved poker almost more than he did bridge. The difference being that you could relax more and have a drink with poker. Parks often said that poker without bourbon was like a whorehouse without women. It just didn't make sense.

Parks had been a fine officer before the booze got to him. Even now he had moments of strength. His bravery under fire and his devotion to his men was never in question. He was a man with a sickness that had been swept under the rug. It was a failing of the military. They took care of their own and hid the weaknesses rather than correcting them. A fondness for liquor was somehow accepted if the person in question could make reveille every morning.

"Dark of the moon tonight, sir." It was the Lt j.g. who was the boat commander who spoke. "Usually means action. This was right about where we were last week when we caught fire from the beach."

"Think they'll try again?" Jack asked.

"Can't be sure. They sometimes hit in the same place three or four times in a row and other times they break off in the middle of a good attack and disappear. Remember that boat last month down south. Drew fire one night and suppressed it. Next night they went in for a look and took a recoilless down the throat."

"Yes," thought Jack. He remembered. "One killed. Two wounded. One missing. One boat out of action for a month." He clicked off the statistics. He knew them. He had counted off those kind of figures too many times.

"Sorry, sir. I didn't mean to imply..."

"Forget it. How far are we off shore?"

"Over a mile, sir. I'm going to work north about another fifteen minutes and then make a run to the shore and back south. Intelligence said they expected activity near here. If we don't turn up any Charlies here, I'll go further north and see if we can spot any junks coming down."

Jack liked the way this man Merryweather talked. He had just been selected for Lieutenant and was finishing up his tour in Viet Nam. This was his last patrol and when it was over he would move to the staff while training his replacement. But right now this was his boat and he had a plan in mind, which he intended to carry out even if the boss was along for the ride. No doubts. No questions. None of the usual "If that's satisfactory with you, sir" crap which always sounded to Jack like the buck being passed back up the line. This young tiger wanted to drag Charlie out of his hole and he wasn't afraid to reach in after him.

"Do you have your orders yet"

"No sir. My relief's orders came in and the X.O. told me to get off the boat ASAP. Other than that, I'm waiting for my next assignment. I'm hoping for a shore tour. Carol and I are getting married as soon as I get home. They can't take my thirty days leave away, so we'll at least have that."

"You went to the Academy, didn't you?

"Yes, sir. Third generation. My old man's a pilot. He was disappointed that I'm not in his footsteps all the way, but grandpa is happy as hell to have a black shoe in the family."

"I envy you, Mr. Merryweather. I'll sure be glad to have this tour behind me. Guess it's too early for me to start clipping links off of my short timers chain."

"Right. Thirty days is the regulation. In fact, Potts, our engineman, tells me that no one over second class petty officer is supposed to have a short timers chain. After that your soul belongs to the navy and you have no business looking forward to anything."

"General Quarters." The Boatswain's Mate passed the word quietly. The boat was turning west, in toward the beach. No sense making a lot of extra noise. It had only turned dark an hour before. The idea was to give the impression that the Swift Boat was heading north. The doubling back wasn't much of a ruse, but then there wasn't much chance for grand strategy with one boat and a big sandy beach between it and old Charlie. If indeed old Charlie was there. This would have normally been a two-boat patrol, but engine trouble aborted the other boat about an hour out of port. Standard procedure would have returned both boats to the base, but Jack had sent a message stating that "unless otherwise directed" they would continue with one boat. No reply from headquarters meant they continued on duties assigned.

The whole boat seemed to come alive. Jack could see the helmeted figures putting on their flak jackets and life preservers. The .50 caliber guns came to life and did their up and down dance as the gunners cocked them and made sure they were free for movement in all directions. Men were opening ammo cans and checking mortar shells.

There was an 81 millimeter mortar mounted under the aft .50 caliber gun. These modern sailors, these men of the nuclear navy, had a muzzle-loading weapon that was aimed and fired like the cannons in John Paul Jones' navy. More sophisticated of course, better range, more hitting power and all that, but in the end you loaded through the muzzle, sighted down the barrel, and fired. Then you waited to see if you hit anything.

"Check those safety wires there, boot." The gunner was needling the newest man in the crew. A fresh faced young sailor just out of boot camp and Swift Boat training.

"Don't worry, you old fart." No shrinking violet this new man. "If these things don't go off it won't be because I screwed up."

"I'm not worried about them not going off, boot. I just don't want the damned things going off in my lap."

Potts, the engineer, stuck his head up out of the engine compartment hatch. "What the hell's the difference? There's nothing in your lap worth worrying about."

"Screw you too, snipe. Back in your pit and make sure those horses don't run out of oats. Stay up here and I'll tell everyone how you crapped your pants last week."

"I was sick. Had the bug. Bent over to throw up and ended up going in my pants. Wasn't my fault. It's the shitty food they feed us. Everything about this place makes me sick."

The banter went on all the time. These men trusted each other, but they remembered an incident with another boat, and this was a light hearted way of going through the check-off list to make sure everyone was ready and nothing was forgotten. They remembered the long search. They remembered seeing a shipmate who had lost an arm and a leg and his eyesight when a mortar round went off in his "lap". They remembered seeing the body of the other man. The one who had the boot's job. He had been in the water three days when they found him. They trusted each other, but they remembered.

"All hands at G.Q., sir." The leading petty officer quietly passed the word on to the skipper that the boat was ready for whatever came.

Ltj.g. Merryweather throttled back the big diesel engines and eased in toward the beach. It was dark. So dark that the stars lighted up the ocean. There was a faint silhouette of the tree line behind the beach just over a mile ahead. The boat moved smoothly forward. The crew felt a slight up and down movement as the boat started to pitch in the mild swells nearer shore. Not much, just a little pitch. When the radar showed eight hundred yards to the shore the skipper eased around to port and headed south. They were closer than five hundred yards he figured because the radar was probably picking up the tree line back off the beach, not the beach itself. His fathometer showed plenty of water under the keel.

"Close enough for government work" he thought to himself.

"Looks quiet enough" Jack whispered. He was thinking of his wife back home and their little boy. The baby was a bit over a year and a half old when he left for Viet Nam. And his wife was pregnant again he found out shortly after arriving in country. Must have been that night they spent gloriously alone at Timber Cove that did it. A smile crossed his lips as he thought about that night with the baby safely boarded at a trusted navy friend's house and a whole week of his fifteen days leave to go. Not a worry in the world. At least there were none that night.

"Light on the beach, sir."

"Where is it, Boats"

"It's off now, but it was broad on the bow. I'm sure of it; no kidding. Like a flashlight. Someone walking." The Boatswain's Mate, or "Boats" as everyone called him, was a good man. And reliable. If he saw a light, it was there.

"Anything through the starlight scope?" The scope was a marvelous instrument that magnified any available light, even that from the stars, and allowed the crew members to "see" in the dark.

"Didn't see anything, but I'm not sure that gizmo is working right tonight."

"Drop in a few mortars, Boats. And I want all three in the air." The idea was to get three rounds off fast from the fairly stable platform the boat presented when moving slowly through the water, then kick the boat in the ass and present a fast moving, difficult target if Charlie was there with a recoilless rocket.

"I'm figuring 900 yards, 15 degrees forward of the beam. Three rounds. Make 'em fast. Shoot." Boats aimed and fired while the seaman loaded. It was good teamwork.

The three rounds went off quickly and as soon as the third one left the barrel the skipper pushed the throttles home and the Swift Boat lived up to her name. They ran about 200 yards until the impact point was just about abeam and then the skipper threw the boat into a tight turn to the left, throttled down and let the boat swing around with the port side facing the beach. The gunners automatically swiveled their .50 calibers around to face the beach. Nothing happened. What was it? Some poor woodsman hiking home after working all day in the jungle forest trying to cut enough burnable wood to sell for a few pennies to buy some rice for just enough energy to go back out tomorrow to cut some more wood? Or some kid playing with a flashlight discarded by an American during the sweep through the area last month? Or was it Charlie signaling to a buddy? Or did Charlie mistake the Swift Boat for the supply junk? Stupid damned war. Even when you see the people shooting at you, there are times you can't believe it. They look so young. Some are women. Some are little kids. You never knew what you were up against.

No one relaxed. All eyes were on the beach. The chances were good that it was Charlie. The area was designated a free fire zone by the Province Chief. The Province Chief is the big man in the area.

He is combination mayor, police chief, father confessor, general, and mafia Don. His word is law. Even the President of the United States can't make anything happen in Viet Nam without going through the Province Chief. The free fire zone designation tells everyone to get out of the area. Anyone found there is automatically designated Viet Cong and is to be shot on sight by friendly troops. The Vietnamese are no different than anyone else and there's always ten percent that don't get the word. A lot innocent people die from a lack of information.

The skipper moved off shore a bit and headed south again. "Guess they don't want to play tonight." He tried to make it an offhand comment, but there was an edge to his voice. A touch of fear was coming to the surface. Everyone felt it. The dryness from breathing through your mouth, the disoriented feeling from staring into the darkness for any sign of movement, the tenseness of every muscle as the adrenalin pumped. You just never know what is going to happen when you start shooting. You walk a fine line between life and death while you're waiting in the darkness for return fire. One of the most traumatizing things about a combat situation is the realization that it is not a drill. There is a fearful comprehension that there are people out there who want to kill you. It's not a movie or a schoolyard fight where you can say "I give" and your opponent lets you up. It's fight or die. Sometimes both. The Gunner put it in terms everyone could understand when he said "My asshole gets sucked up around my belly button every time."

Jack lapsed back into the quiet reverie that was all his own and far away from the war. Back to Timber Cove and Sally. Then he thought about their trip to Disneyland later on and quick thoughts of an argument over some insignificant thing popped into his mind and before he knew it his thoughts took him to that familiar subject, his last night before leaving for Viet Nam. They did everything in a normal every evening fashion. After the baby was in bed Jack mixed a jug of martinis and he and Sally sat and talked about small things. After a while, Sally got out the salad and put on the finishing touches. "My favorite salad, honey. What's the occasion?" That wasn't exactly the right thing to say, but it passed quickly. The dinner was perfect. Candlelight and wine. Holding hands across the table. A most romantic evening. They went to bed early and talked. Nothing else, just talk. Jack had tried a couple of caresses. Sally hadn't tried to stop him, but it just wasn't right. It just wasn't an evening for making love. For being in love, yes, but not for making love. There was more to this night. There was a deep feeling between them as they lay there in the beach front cottage that they had rented for the period that Jack went though special training before going overseas. They held hands and were very quiet. There wasn't anything to talk about. They were facing twelve months of separation. Maybe an eternity.

The explosion took on a life of its own. The whole boat lighted up and the noise was terrible. Jack felt himself spinning slightly and he could see Sally's face. And there was the baby. Why were they making so much noise? Why were they pouring that wine in his mouth? What kind of party was this anyway? Then he felt something tugging at him. A far away voice was calling. Damned fool young officers making all that noise, why couldn't they come into the BOQ quietly and go to bed like normal human beings? Why did they have to yell and tug and pour things on people. He felt warm all over, like sitting in a tub of bath water. What the hell is going on here? Jack could feel himself being dragged over some boards. He heard voices but nothing made sense. The pain centered in his stomach and felt like he was going to throw up. Then euphoria calmed his body like a soothing massage as he slipped into peaceful darkness.

CHAPTER 4

Back to the west Jeff Dunlay was coming out of his dark place. His leg hurt. He had been injured playing football, and he had been in fights, but this was something he had never experienced before. His whole body was feeling the pain in his foot. The V.C. soldiers were pulling him away from the pit he had stepped into. There was bone-jarring agony as one of the V.C. pulled the bamboo out of his foot. He somehow held on to consciousness. Jeff kept his eyes squeezed shut during the torture. He was afraid of what he would see when he opened them, but he was alive and he wasn't going to give up while he still had breath to fight. There were fifteen V.C. guerillas in their black pajamas standing around him. He could see a few others stripping the corpses of Kiley and Smolen. They took everything including their shorts and socks. The only one paying any attention to Jeff was the pleasant looking young fellow tying a dirty rag around his foot. Jeff started to reach for his foot and realized that his hands were tied behind his back. He was a prisoner. He was hurt and might not be able to walk. There may not be a tomorrow for him. Then a thought came to him: "Good thing the lieutenant didn't wait to promote me. Whatever happens, I'll be drawing corporal's pay."

Jeff looked for a way to escape but he didn't have much time for thinking. The head man of the V.C. group motioned for him to get up and start walking. Jeff made it to his feet and to his surprise found that he could walk. How could that be? He had heard about punji stakes. He had seen a man brought back from the jungle who had stepped on one. By all rights he should be expecting to have his foot cut off right now. Maybe it was a small stake with no dung smeared on it to promote infection. Whatever the answer was, he could walk. The Charlies let him keep his boots. The young fellow had forced his boot back on after tying the rag around his foot. There was another problem. When they roughly helped him to his feet he felt a bad pain in his side. Jeff remembered stepping on the punji stake and then being knocked down. It was like being hit by the biggest linebacker in the league. Maybe that was why he was still alive. His flack jacket had taken the force of the bullet that knocked him down and when he went down and stayed down the V.C. stopped shooting. Flak jackets worked, but you still end up with a hefty bruise and sometimes a broken rib or two.

He wasn't in good shape, but he was walking. If he could keep walking he had a chance. Jeff got one last look at Kiley and Smolen and it made him sick. The flies were all over their naked bodies. That was no way to leave a man. He couldn't see the village or what happened to the rest of the platoon. This group that had captured him were professionals, not some rag-tag, half starved bunch of local V.C. conscripts. Escape was Jeff's first thought, but it wasn't going to be a cakewalk. Boy, if his little brother could see him now. Wonder what he'd say. Probably some smart assed remark like "You got what you had coming to you, big brother." No his little brother wouldn't say anything like that. Oh, hell, what's the difference, "I've got to get out of this" thought Jeff.

But it wasn't going to end. Not for some time. For two days Jeff was pushed, pulled and dragged through the jungle forest. Always heading north. North by east really. He had been treated well enough. His foot hurt, but amazingly no infection had set in. He did have a roaring case of the runs, which brought him no sympathy from his captors. The runs were a way of life for them. He couldn't seem to coordinate his biological needs with the rest stops. It was embarrassing, but no one seemed to mind except him. On the third day of his capture, Jeff was led into a small hamlet almost identical to the one where this nightmare started. He was shoved into a small mud and straw room. The door was closed, and except for a streak of light near the roof, it was dark.

★ ★ ★

Jack Walker woke up with someone shaking him violently. His chest hurt and his ears were ringing, but when he was dragged to his feet he found that nothing seemed broken. He could see, and except for the ringing in his ears he could hear. His hands were tied behind his back and a noose was around his neck. "What's happening? Where's the rest of the crew? What's going on here?" A hard slap across his mouth shut him up. He started to look around but someone yanked his noose and almost pulled him back to the ground. Seconds later he was in the jungle trotting along behind several men in black pajamas.

What were the statistics? Six killed? One missing and presumed captured? Would he ever know? The rest of the crew must be dead or they would be here too. Maybe not, maybe they were taken someplace else. Maybe the boat got away. Not likely. They wouldn't have left him there in the water. The pain in his chest grew worse and he was thirsty. Bad, bad cotton in the mouth thirsty. But the little men ahead of him didn't seem to care and he wasn't going to look behind him again. They almost broke his neck the last time.

If Jack had been able to see back to the time his boat was hit he would have seen that his guess at the statistics was dead right. There had been several shells fired at the boat. The first one hit amidships and exploded just behind the pilot house. That was the one that knocked Jack into the water. Ltjg Merryweather caught the full impact and died almost immediately. His body had shielded Jack from the blast. The second shell hit aft by the gun mount and set off a box of mortars. The crew back there never finished the argument they were having about whether it was better to be from South Carolina or New Jersey. It would never make a difference to them again. The engineman went down with the boat, trapped in the pit where he was checking the engines, as did the quartermaster who was below bringing up more ammunition. The radioman who was on the forward mount had been hit by shrapnel but he had been able to hoist Jack up on the wooden floorboards that floated to the surface from the pilot house. The radioman had no idea how badly he had been hurt and he died from a loss of blood shortly after helping Jack.

The pace along the trail was steady but not so fast that Jack couldn't keep up. He let his mind wander to other thoughts. He was wishing he could sit down with someone and have a good bull session right now. Back at the base it was his favorite off-duty pastime. Jack had inherited a refrigerator with his room in the living quarters. He kept it stocked with beer and there was never any problem getting people to accept an invitation to come in and swap lies. Fixcue, of the St. Louis Quincy's, was one of his favorites; the young j.g. had a philosophical quality and he loved a good controversy.

One of their most compelling discussions was the night they got on the subject of bravery and cowardice. It started innocently enough with some comments about crewmembers that had acted heroically in tough situations. The conversation got serious when Jack observed that back in civilian life if a person kills, he would probably end up in jail. At the very least his actions will be carefully examined and he will escape jail only if he can justify what he did. But the same man, in the war in Viet Nam, may go to jail for failing to kill. Cowardice is a military crime.

Fixcue thought that was just fine, as did the Supply Officer and "Brick" Schwartz, the Maintenance Officer. Brick was his usual eloquent self after a few beers. "Any cocksucker can't cut it, fuck him."

Jack hadn't thought too deeply on the subject until then, but now that there was a chance for a good argument he immediately took the side of the cowards of the world. He shoved his beer can in Fixcue's face and challenged him. "Where the hell is it written that a man can't be a coward?"

"In the Uniform Code of Military Justice. The fucking UCMJ, that's where. There gonna be no fucking cowards in my navy." Brick had taken up the challenge while Fixcue was wiping off the beer that Jack had spilled all over him.

"I mean where is it written by normal people. The UCMJ is nothing normal humans deal with. I mean where is it written in places like the Ten Commandments, or the Golden Rule, or the Constitution of the United States?" This time Jack punctuated his challenge by spilling beer on all three of his guests.

Fixcue regained his composure. "How can you run a military organization if you have cowards involved? If a man joins the navy he should understand that he is apt to go in harm's way."

"But what about the people who get drafted?"

"They still take the oath. That's the way it is."

"So a guy can be an atheist, a communist, a Baptist, a machinist, a total bore, an intellectual, a drunk, a bum, a hard worker, or any other god damned thing he wants to be, but he can't be a coward. Who the hell made that rule? Who made it a crime?"

Brick again rose to the occasion. "If no one else made it, I made the rule. No cocksucker is gonna be a coward in my navy."

Fixcue got out of his chair and stood menacingly in front of Jack. The argument had taken on some meaning for him. "Any crime is abhorrent, but cowardice is the supreme insult to humanity. The coward puts himself above everyone else in importance. No one, nothing, is worth his sacrifice. The coward thinks only of himself. He deserves our ridicule. He deserves our condemnation."

"That's what I would have fucking said if I went to college." Brick was standing next to Fixcue and the two of them were jabbing Jack in the chest with beer cans. They pushed him halfway across the room until he got tangled up with a chair and a garbage can and fell sprawling in the floor laughing.

"I drink to the cowards of the world." Jack raised his beer can to his mouth, but it was empty. He went to the reefer for another can, but it was empty too. "To hell with it. And to hell with all you damned drunks. You come in here, drink all my beer, argue with me about everything in the fucking world and you don't even know what the hell you're talking about. I'm going to bed."

And so ended the great debate. That was just talk. Out here on the trail with an enemy squad of soldiers was reality. They had trekked for two days and finally Jack was led into a clearing. Just beyond was a hamlet of mud and straw huts. He was led to one of the huts and roughly shoved through the door. As he stumbled into the dark he tripped over something and heard a moan. Then a voice: "What are you bastards up to now?" It was another American. Jack was so thirsty he could barely speak but he managed to squeak out "Lieutenant Jack Walker, U.S. Navy."

"Corporal Geoffrey Dunlay, United States Marine Corps, sir." came the reply out of the darkness.

Jack felt something wet at his lips and he grabbed at the rag Jeff had soaked in water for him. After he got some moisture he asked for a real drink.

"Take it easy, sir. Not too much all at once."

"It's o.k. Corporal, I'll take it easy."

After a few minutes Jack felt like he could talk again. "Guess I got here just in time, Corporal. Looks like they had you surrounded."

It broke the ice and for the first time in three days Jeff managed a grin.

"Any more good guys around, Corporal? Or are we the only ones in this rat hole?"

"Couldn't tell you, sir. I haven't been here long, but they've had me in this hut. Haven't heard anything that sounded like other Americans. They haven't paid much attention to me, and they don't have an interpreter here or he would have been around by now."

Jack was impressed with his hut mate. He thought to himself: This is a good marine to be with in a spot like this. They could barely see each other in the dark but Jeff Dunlay came through loud and clear.

"I think you're right, Corporal. And they wouldn't have us together if their brass were here. Were you operating near here?"

"No, sir. I'm not sure where we are right now, but we hiked a lot of miles from our position to get here."

"I know we can't be more than twenty miles from the coast." Jack was estimating the time he spent on the trail and how far he could have traveled through the jungle terrain during that time. He had to estimate because his watch now belonged to Charlie.

"Good God, sir. If you're right I must be at least 30 or 40 miles from where my outfit got hit. We were pretty far inland. I wonder why they went to all the trouble of hauling me here? I've got a punji stake, or at least the hole from one, in my foot. They could have left me there and I probably would have died from fright."

Fat chance of this fellow being that frightened, thought Jack. "I was wondering the same thing. They knocked my boat out and I was in the water. They had to go out a quarter of a mile from shore to drag me in. They must want prisoners for some reason."

The door opened and a small man in black pajamas pushed some bowls into the room. There was a little bit of rice in each bowl and some stuff that looked like grass. That was all they could see before the door closed.

"Feel up to eating something, sir?"

"Pass it over. As long as they are feeding us they aren't going to shoot us. We have a chance to get out of here."

Young Dunlay passed the bowl of rice and whatever else was in the bowl over to Jack and they ate in silence. The rice tasted like rice and the grass tasted like grass. It was the little hard things that they didn't want to talk about. Nothing in the bowl tasted bad, but it was probably better that the room was dark.

"Do you have any water over there?" Jack was still thirsty and the spice in the bowl of food added to the thirst.

"Yes, sir. One thing we have is plenty of water. They put a big jug of it in here with us. Must be near a river or something. It tastes like pretty good water and they aren't stingy with it."

As the two Americans were falling asleep following their meal, Jack thought: "Thank God. At least I'm not alone in this mess. Maybe between the two of us we can get out of here and back to the coast."

CHAPTER 5

Sally Walker went to the door in a very irritated mood and mumbling to herself, "Why the hell do people have to come calling when I'm either sleeping, in the shower, or feeding the baby?" She had been feeding the baby; or rather watching him feed himself with all the confidence of a two year old. In the mouth, on the floor and on the wall all in one motion -- very quickly, and with no malice intended. Eating was fun for the baby, but not for Sally. Every meal was sheer torture for her and some idiot salesman or neighbor banging on the door didn't help. When Sally opened the door there was a Navy Lieutenant Commander standing there and Sally knew immediately that Jack was in trouble. "Yes, what is it?"

"I'm Lieutenant Commander Karpaski." He showed his identification card. "Are you Mrs. Sally Walker, wife of Lieutenant John Walker?"

Sally felt faint, but she had never fainted in her life. That was something they did in the movies. She just didn't know what to do.

"Yes, I'm Sally Walker."

"May I come in, please, Mrs. Walker. I have some information concerning your husband."

"Please come in and have a seat in the living room. I have to check the baby. Can I get you a cup of coffee?" Sally didn't want to hear the words. She knew it was bad or the officer wouldn't be there in person. But it was only one officer. No Chaplain. That was good. She took the baby out of his chair and carried him into the living room amid much protesting and screaming about the unfinished meal. Sally put Todd in the corner with some toys to distract him and turned to the officer. "What is it Commander? Is my husband dead?" The words were so dry that Sally couldn't believe it was her talking.

"We hope not, Mrs. Walker. The Navy Department has word that your husband is missing. He was on a boat that was sunk. This isn't pleasant, but it might give you some hope. Everyone else on the boat was killed and all the bodies were found in the boat or washed up on the shore. Your husband wasn't found. There's a good chance he was taken prisoner, but we can't be sure."

"Thank you, Commander. Would you like some coffee?" She was acting like she had just been told that the electricity had been turned off and would be back on in ten minutes. She just couldn't comprehend what she had been told. Jack had been missing for almost seven months. Missing from home. Missing from her life, but she had known that he could be reached and he was safe. Now he was really missing. He was lost. She couldn't send him a telegram or have the Red Cross contact him. He couldn't telephone her like he did on her birthday two months ago. He was missing.

Sally stood up suddenly and went into the kitchen. She dampened a towel and held it to her face. Then she heard the baby crying and it all came alive for her. This was real and Jack was missing. She slumped into a chair and buried her face in the towel. She heard Lieutenant Commander Karpaski come into the kitchen.

"I'll be all right, Commander. Sorry for leaving you like that." Karpaski took a seat across the table from her. They sat there for a few minutes. There wasn't anything to say, but he felt that he should at least stay until he was sure she was composed.

Karpaski thought to himself that he would rather be shot than have to notify families about things like this. There just isn't any easy way to tell a wife that her husband is missing, or worse yet, dead. This was the twenty-sixth CACO call he had made. The life of the Casualty Assistance Calls Officer, CACO in navy language, is bleak at best. The navy sends an officer out in every casualty case to personally notify the next of kin. It is an extra duty assigned to an officer or group of officers in a geographical area. Generally it goes to the lowest ranking, most inexperienced officer in the area because everyone knew what a lousy job it was to tell family members that someone they loved was either dead, badly injured, or missing altogether. No one wanted the job. Tony Karpaski was the commanding officer of a Reserve Training Center and by virtue of rank should have been immune from CACO calls, but a quirk of geography made him the only officer available in his particular area. He was the only naval officer for many miles around so every casualty notification in his area fell to him and he had to do it alone.

Sally got up and went into the living room and came back carrying the baby. Her eyes were red. She was pale, but she had a little smile on her face. It was easy to see that she was using every ounce of her will to keep her attention focused on the baby until she could get the pill down that her husband was missing.

"That offer for coffee still goes, Commander. I'll try to do better this time."

"Please don't go to any trouble on my account, Mrs. Walker." Karpaski was balancing on the edge of a knife. He didn't want to impose any more that necessary, but he didn't want to rush off until he felt everything was stable.

"No trouble, Commander. I'd appreciate it if you would join me for a cup. I won't keep you long, but right now the sight of that uniform helps."

"In that case, I'd love a cup. Could I get it? Looks like you have your hands full with that little fellow."

"If you don't mind. It's all made. The baby didn't get to finish his dinner. I'll give him his desert while you pour the coffee."

Karpaski poured the coffee and sat in the chair against the wall. Sally got the baby settled down and joined him at the table. "Are you married, Commander?"

"Sure am. I have three kids. We live out in Clinton. It's about twenty miles east of here."

"I'm sorry you have to be away from your family. This can't be pleasant duty for you."

"Please don't worry about me. I'm with my family and grateful for it. You're the one with the problem. I want you to know that you can call on me any time of the day or night to help you. Any time, anything. You call me. Your husband would do the same for my family if our situations were reversed."

They talked for a while longer. Karpaski was impressed with Sally. As much as he hated CACOs, it was much easier when the people he called on could keep things in perspective. He had seen all kinds of people in these situations and some were very unpleasant, even going so far as to blame him for the death of their loved one.

After the Commander had gone, Sally was alone with her thoughts. And she had never felt so alone in her life, so dismally, utterly alone. She recalled what Jack had said before he left. He had just completed his training and was getting ready to go overseas. Part of his training had been in survival and also in what to do if taken prisoner by the enemy. He had said, "Don't worry, honey. Nothing is going to keep me from coming back to you. And if you get word that I have been wounded or captured, don't worry. I'll be back." Sally believed those words now. They were her corner stone. He would be back. He had to come back.

CHAPTER 6

Jack and Jeff were awakened by shouting and running outside their hut. They could hear gunshots in the distance, but it didn't sound like a fire fight. More like probing. It was almost too much to think about, but if friendly patrols were in the area there was a chance of rescue, or a possibility of escape.

Suddenly the door burst open and four men in black pajamas came into the hut. They jabbed the prisoners with their rifles and indicated for them to stand up. They pulled their hands roughly behind their backs and tied them with coarse ropes. Then a noose was slipped over each of their heads and they were shoved out of the hut. It was near sunset, but the brightness of the sky was blinding after the darkness in the hut. When Jack fell, he was prodded in the stomach with a rifle barrel. Jeff winced, his side still hurt badly. He was almost sure he had a cracked rib; a punch in the side would cripple him so he stood quietly, unable to help. Jack got to his feet as fast as he could, but he wasn't quite fast enough to keep from getting his leash yanked.

Jeff was doing fairly well in spite of his sore foot and hurt rib. He managed to stay upright. He wanted to help the lieutenant, but there wasn't anything he could do. Neither Jack nor Jeff talked, nor did they show any more emotion than they could help. The idea of the game was to be as bland as possible. Don't resist too much. Don't help at all. Don't smile, and above all, don't show anger. When someone has your hands tied behind your back and a rifle stuck in your gut there is little to be accomplished by making faces at him. Play it cool and hope for the chance to escape.

A half a dozen soldiers came running into the clearing. They were young, early twenties, but they had the hard look of veterans. One man, a bit older than the rest, seemed to be in charge. He gave several orders. Two of the soldiers went back into the jungle in the direction that the shots had come from earlier. The rest of them headed off in the opposite direction dragging Jack and Jeff along. They were heading northwest as best Jack could tell by the sun, and that wasn't good. After walking for about two hours the group stopped. No one paid much attention to the two Americans as they sat down next to one another.

"Where do you think they're taking us?" asked Jeff.

"They're taking us north and that's bad. The further north we go the closer we get to the border. We've got to get away from these guys or we're going to spend a long time with them."

None of the soldiers seemed to mind the talking. One of them filled a cup and gave each of the prisoners a drink. It was pretty certain by this time that none of the soldiers spoke English, or even French. There was no way for the prisoners to find out what was happening to them.

The two soldiers who had gone off earlier caught up with the group. They were smiling and they pointed back to where they had come from. There had been a short skirmish with some South Vietnamese Army troops. It didn't take much to discourage the ARVN soldiers. Sometimes the VC put up signs that said "Mine Field, Keep Out." Or more boldly, a sign saying "Viet Cong Territory." It was often enough to turn the ARVN troops back. An armed attack was even more convincing. They told their story to the leader who was watching Jack and Jeff. The leader smiled and motioned for everyone to get up and start moving. Jeff started to say something, but before he had said three words he was slapped hard across the mouth and had a rifle muzzle stuck up under his chin. Evidently it was permitted to talk during the breaks, but on the trail it was silent going. There was a red mark on Jeff's face, but he wasn't hurt by the blow. His mind offered a short prayer of thanks that he hadn't been punched in the ribs. They were being taught the rules and the game wasn't fun. They started back the same way from where they had come earlier.

★ ★ ★

Something woke Phil Dunlay. He couldn't place it for a minute. Then he realized that his wife was crying. He was worried about his wife. She had been crying almost constantly since the telegram came. "Anita, it won't do any good to keep crying. Remember that officer who came to talk to us right after the telegram came? He said 'Jeff is missing'. The chances are very good that he is alive and will make his way back to his unit. You mustn't think of him as dead." He put his hand on his wife's shoulder, but she pulled away.

"Don't touch me, Phil, ever again." The words cut like a razor.

"Are you awake, Anita?"

"Yes, I'm awake. And I don't want you to touch me. You sent our boy off to that damned war. You signed those papers. It was you and that judge who killed my son. He would have been better off in jail. At least he would be alive."

"Good God, Anita, you can't be serious. We don't know that he might be dead, and besides, I couldn't have stopped him from joining up. He would have done it on his own, lied about his age, or just waited another month until he was eighteen." Phil was really jolted. He had no idea that his wife blamed him for Jeff being lost. He tried again to take his wife's hand. Anita got up quietly, took her pillow and a blanket and moved into the guest room.

Phil lay there in a daze. "What in the hell is happening?" he thought. One son missing in a war, the other one travelling around with a bunch of political lunatics, and his wife blaming him for the whole thing. And his daughter, what about his daughter? What the hell kind of trouble was she getting into?

Phil needn't have worried about his daughter. She was spending most of her spare time at the navy hospital as a volunteer worker with the Red Cross. Of course, Phil would have found something to worry about if his daughter had been in a convent. She was a pretty girl, and popular. There seemed to be a different boy every week. Phil started worrying when Susie had her first date.

There was only one solution to the events of this day. Phil got out of bed and went downstairs to the liquor cabinet and poured himself a stiff shot of whiskey. When the sun came up Phil was sitting in his easy chair. The whiskey bottle was empty and he felt terrible. He wasn't drunk, but he was tired and he was cold. Then he became terribly ill. He made it to the bathroom and after an eternity of painful retching he gave up every ounce of whiskey he had drunk. Then he went back to bed. "Screw it" he thought. "I'll never get out of bed again."

★ ★ ★

In the jungle it was pitch black; Jack and Jeff were being dragged along by their necks. They were scratched and cut from branches and rocks, and they were tired. Jeff was exhausted and his foot hurt, but Jack was in real pain. He was sure he was going to die and almost afraid he wouldn't. His legs were buckling under him every other step and his heart was hammering. The ringing in his ears was even painful, and his head was spinning.

Every day back at the staff office Jack had promised himself that this was the day he would start getting back in shape. Some exercises. Some jogging. But there was never enough time. Now he was paying for the soft life behind that desk. The only thing that kept him going was the fear of another kick or punch.

When they broke into the clearing Jack recognized it as the place they had been earlier in the day. There was a cooking fire burning just beyond the hut which was their prison, and he could hear a small stream running further beyond the fire. He looked up at the stars to get a bearing. It was instinct more than anything else. He thought to himself, "What the hell difference does it make. I couldn't get away if they sent a cab for me."

The soldiers cut Jack and Jeff's ropes and directed them into the hut. They didn't have the energy to shove them through the door in the usual rough manner. Even the soldiers were pooped out. Jack stumbled through the door and passed out on the mud floor. Jeff shook him and tried to wake him up. The door had been left ajar and the soldiers were over on the other side of the compound. It was a chance to get away. Not much of a chance, but possibly the only one they would ever get. They had been told in survival school to be alert for a chance to get away. You have to be ready all the time. There won't be many chances. When it comes take it. Move boldly. Jeff shook Jack again. He even poured some water on him, but it was no use. Now the question was: should he try to make it alone? Leave the officer here? It was the only chance. It was his duty to escape. If he made it, he could get help and come back for the lieutenant.

Jeff got down on the floor of the hut and peeked around the corner of the door. No one was watching the hut. He slithered out and got the hut between him and the soldiers and headed for the jungle. He had no plan other than to get away from the hamlet. He made it to the edge of the clearing and then into the jungle. He was going to make it. Jeff moved quietly in a half crouch. He felt branches pulling at his torn clothes, and when he put his foot down it sounded to him like he was playing a drum solo. If he could just get a bit further into the jungle before the soldiers noticed he was gone.

One of the pajama-clad soldiers noticed that the door to the hut was open. He walked over and looked in. He saw Jack lying there and evidently assumed that Jeff was further back in the hut in the darkness. He closed the door.

Jeff pushed on until almost daybreak. He was sure he was moving east, toward the coast. He had no idea how far he had traveled when he came to with the sun in his eyes. It could have been a couple of miles or a couple of hundred yards. He had had to feel his way in the dark and kept banging into trees and branches. At each clear spot he would look up and check the stars for a bearing. He was heading east. He stepped on something soft that writhed and hissed. It was a snake for sure, but what kind? How big? Poisonous? He couldn't tell and in the dark he had no idea where it was. In the blackness of the jungle Jeff panicked. He was exhausted and thirsty. His muscles ached and he was scared beyond belief. He was alone in a jungle with a snake. Jeff started to run. Every bush and tree branch became a writhing serpent, every root he stepped on felt deadly. He lost all control. Perhaps it saved his life when he ran headlong into a tree and he knocked himself unconscious where he lay until the sun woke him.

At daybreak, the guard opened the door to the hut and saw that there was only one prisoner there. He sounded the alarm and several soldiers ran to the hut. The older man, the one in charge, looked in the door and then closed it.

The noise of orders being barked and people running outside woke Jack up. He listened for a minute and then in a hoarse whisper called out "Corporal, where are you?" There was no answer. He started feeling around the floor of the hut. The marine wasn't there. Outside the shouting continued and he could hear the soldiers running in different directions and calling to each other. At first, Jack thought that the VC had taken Jeff outside for some reason. But why all the running around and shouting? Then it hit him. "That son of a bitch, he had a chance to escape and he left me here. How could he do that?" Jack tried to stand up and he realized how sore and weak he was. "Is that what happened? He couldn't wake me up. Oh, my God. I had a chance to escape and didn't make it." Lieutenant Jack Walker slumped back down on the mud floor in a sea of self-pity and cried.

Jeff was flat on his back and the sun was bright in his face. His head felt like it was in a vise. There was a big lump on his forehead and dried blood had caked on his face and around his eyes. He couldn't open his eyes at first and panic gripped him again. "I'm blind." Then he rubbed his eyes and slowly got them open. The sight that greeted him was like the Promised Land. He was looking down a valley and far in the distance he thought he could make out the blue of the South China Sea. Now the months of training and discipline took over. "Don't blow it now, Jeff boy. Think. Use your head. Get organized. If Charlie was anywhere nearby that ocean might as well be a thousand miles away. If you start thrashing around and do something stupid you'll be back in the hut. If they catch you again you'll get the ass kicking of your life. If they don't kill you."

From his vantage point Jeff could see what appeared to be a trail below him winding through the jungle. He knew that was a luxury he would have to forego. He would have to make it to the sea the hard way. The trails belonged to Charlie. It would be slow going and once he got to the coast there was no guarantee that he would find friendly forces. But the lieutenant had come from the sea and he had been aboard a boat and that boat was on a regular patrol. It was his only chance. Jeff started down the incline. Once he left the high point he was in deep jungle. At times it closed over him like an umbrella. There were beautiful flowers and thick branches and vines, and anywhere he looked a thousand different species were fighting for the sunlight. His jungle boots were ripped and torn. Maybe it was a good thing. If they had been in good condition some V.C. might have taken them. The little bastards would have to put both feet in one boot to fill it, he thought. At least they provided protection, but his foot was starting to hurt where the punji stake had gone through it. "Oh, shit," thought Jeff. "Don't get infected now."

When he woke up it was almost cool. The night had driven out some of the intense jungle heat. But now it was warming up, getting hot with the morning sun. The jungle gets hot like no other place on earth. It gets under your skin and behind your eyeballs. It bakes your bones and boils the water out of your body. Jeff remembered from somewhere in high school that the human body is 75% water. He busied himself with vague mental calculations as he stumbled through the growth and determined that at his present rate of perspiration he would weigh about four and a half pounds by the end of the day. He found a stump with water in it. There were little animals in the water. Jeff took a leaf and fashioned a cup for himself. He tried to strain out the little animals but realized that it wasn't the guys that you could see that gave you the roaring drizzles. In survival school they said you could live on insects. They contained lots of protein. There was little choice and Jeff took in the living protein with the water. He made a point of drinking all the water he could hold. Then he took off his boot and inspected his foot. It was turning red and there was pus around the hole on the bottom of his foot. He tried to wash it off as best he could. Then he rinsed the ragged bandage and wrapped it around the wound again and forced his boot back on. He took another drink. His body ached to lie down and sleep, but he forced himself up and started through the foliage again.

Without even realizing it Jeff found himself on a trail and walking with relative ease. The sun was high in sky and unmerciful. Jeff felt terrible. His foot was throbbing and his head hurt. Everything hurt. He was scratched and bruised. Worst of all he was dirty. He was filthy and he smelled. Not the smell of a hard day's work; he stank like something out of a rotten sewer. The mosquitoes and flies and waves of unidentifiable things chewed on him constantly. He wondered how they stood the smell.

The sun and heat got to be too much and Jeff realized that he was making a bad mistake walking on a trail. He crawled back into the jungle and slumped down in a little patch of grass that felt like a feather bed. He wasn't far off of the trail but no one on the trail would know he was there even if he did a dance behind the green curtain. As he slipped in and out of consciousness he thought to himself that he was glad he couldn't wake the lieutenant. Probably would have had to carry the old fart all the way to the ocean. Then he felt guilty for even thinking such things. That was a fellow American back there. What punishment would he have to endure because of Jeff's escape?

That V.C. head man would see to it that someone paid the price. Besides, marines weren't supposed to think ill of officers. Maybe he had better concentrate on the sergeant that sweet-talked him into this mess in the first place. Sergeant Emil Kline. That son of a bitch could take his glory, tradition, and chest full of medals and shove them up his ass.

It was a fitful sleep and when he woke up he thought he was back in the hut. There were voices. They sure as hell weren't American. They were about thirty feet away. Jeff could tell by the sun that he hadn't dozed more than an hour or so. It was even hotter than when he holed up. Who were they? There was no chance they were friendly. He was a dead man if anyone saw him. The V.C. didn't have ammo to waste, but if they saw an American coming out of the jungle they would shoot first and ask questions later.

Back in the grass hut, Jack was having his own troubles. His captors were madder than hell about Jeff getting away and that put Jack in a particularly bad position. The older man had slapped the rest of the squad around unmercifully for letting one of the Americans escape and the whole bunch was in a mean mood. Jack had been dragged out into the clearing and knocked to his knees. The older man had stood in front of him and screamed at him. He was obviously demanding to know where the other American was, but Jack couldn't understand what he was saying. Even if he answered, no one would know what he was talking about. Not only that, he didn't know any more about what had happened to Jeff than the rest of them. Thank God for that. If nothing else, he didn't have to worry about cracking under questioning and causing the death of a shipmate. "Man, that propaganda they fed us in survival school really took hold" thought Jack.

The V.C. finally realized what Jack already knew. They weren't going to communicate and they had better figure out some other way to get the other American back. The orders were out to take as many prisoners as possible. A big offensive was being planned. The prisoners would be the focus of the negotiation talks to throw the Americans off stride. All this strategy was beyond the scope of the little band holding Jack, but like hundreds of other small units, they were following orders. The leader had sent a report that he had two prisoners. Now he only had one. That would have to be explained.

The water jug had been removed from the hut and even the simple straw mat that had been on the floor had been removed. There were no offers of food either. Jack tried to think of Sally and tried to will his mind to communicate with her through telepathy. He wanted her to know that he was alive and in pretty good shape, all things considered. In shape? Dammit, if he had kept himself in shape he'd be out there with the corporal right now. If the corporal had only been able to wake him up. If only they had been able to see the V.C. on the beach before the boat got hit. If, if, if. If he had followed general rule number one and never volunteered for this stupid duty he'd be sitting on his fat backside back in the States right now on shore duty. He had earned it. Almost six years of sea duty, and a tour in D.C. He was a shoe-in for Lieutenant Commander when the list came out next year. He would have been just as much of a shoe-in if he had taken the shore assignment with the CruDesPac staff. He could have been prancing around conducting surprise inspections on hapless destroyer crews during the day and sitting at home in the evening.

Once again Jack had let his mind wander and he forgot where he was for a moment. He was annoyed at the interruption when the door burst open and a new face appeared.

"Good afternoon, Lieutenant. I hope you are comfortable." The voice had the peculiar accent of the Vietnamese speaking English, but the words were fluent.

Jack almost answered, but then he remembered the day he had spent in the mock prisoner of war camp before coming overseas. He looked at the face but kept his own expression bland. What the hell were the rules? Name, rank, service number, and religion. No! Not religion. Place of birth. No! Date of birth. That was it. Name, rank and place of birth. Oh, God, they had told him about this too. "You'll be weak and hungry. Maybe you'll be wounded. You will be no match for them so don't try to play the smart guy. Just give your name, rank, service number and date of birth." That was it. Date of birth. O.K. Try not to say anything. Be noncommittal. Play stupid; that was best. Let them think they captured the dumbest lieutenant in the U.S. Navy. There shouldn't be any physical torture unless you provoke them. Keep quiet. Don't say anything.

The face smiled. "Lieutenant, you don't have any water." There was a rush of Vietnamese and a soldier came running in with the water jug. "Please have a drink. It is hot in here."

Jack took a long drink. There were no rules that said you had to die of thirst.

"Now tell me, Lieutenant, what happened to your marine friend? The sergeant outside is quite embarrassed about his getting away." Jack looked straight into the smiling face, but he said nothing.

"Did your friend just leave you behind? Why didn't you go together? You aren't wounded are you, Lieutenant?"

This was like some goddamned movie he had seen somewhere, sometime in another life. Was this situation real with the smiling, polite oriental giving him water and asking about his health?

"Lieutenant, do not tell me you are going to give me that name, rank, service number jazz. You can talk to me. I know who you are and where you come from. You are Lieutenant John Walker, Operations Officer of the Northern Coastal Swift Boat Squadron. Your squadron call sign is Pepsodent Papa. You have fourteen PCFs in you squadron and two of them are in the shipyard for overhaul. You were making one of your usual unauthorized trips in Papa 118. I know all about you. I knew about you when you arrived in my country seven months ago. I am not trying to get any military secrets from you. I just want to be your friend and make a good communist out of you." The smile widened and the face laughed.

"Good grief," thought Jack. "He has the script. This is exactly what they told us would happen."

"Are you waiting for the bamboo under the fingernails, Lieutenant? Shall I torture you and find out what size skivvies your admiral in Saigon wears?"

Jack tried to keep a bland expression, but he was almost on the verge of laughing at the situation. He was also on the verge of wetting his pants. He had no idea what was coming next. These people could kill him at a whim and no one in the world would know what happened. This was no game. He might die right here.

"You have no information I want, Lieutenant Walker. Let us be friends. Frankly, this is R & R for me, a good chance to catch up on the latest American idiom. We're going to move you up north soon, but I was sent to find out what happened to the other American."

"Right by the script," thought Jack. "This is ridiculous."

"Have you had anything to eat, Lieutenant? We don't have steak and french fries to offer, but Vietnamese food is nourishing and quite tasty. Let me have some sent in."

The smiling face called for the guard and gave several quick orders. Jack's head was becoming a little clearer. If he could just keep his wits about him and not get tricked or provoked into talking, everything would be o.k.

"Tell me your name, Lieutenant. You must, you know. The Geneva Convention rules say you must."

"My name is Jack Walker."

"The rest of it, Lieutenant Walker, please. Don't you remember? Name, rank, service number and date of birth, please."

"Lieutenant John Phillip Walker. 573137. 26 March 1938."

But, Lieutenant, you just said that your name was Jack Walker. Now you tell me it is John Phillip Walker. Tell me again, Lieutenant, what is your real name?"

"Dammit," thought Jack. "The first time I open my mouth, I have to screw up. Now he has me going. I'm going to have to answer him but he knows I'm rattled. He isn't going to let up until he gets me to make another mistake."

"Lieutenant, tell me your correct name. If you lie to me I can have you shot as a spy."

"John Phillip Walker."

"No, no, no, Lieutenant, the whole thing, name, rank, service number and date of birth. How do I know that you did not lie to me about that too? Maybe you are not an officer. Maybe it was the officer who escaped. Is that not the way you do things in your country? What is the expression? Rank has its privilege. Tell me again, Lieutenant."

"Wow!" thought Jack. "This guy's an expert. I haven't said twenty words and he already has enough evidence to shoot me. He won't even be sure who it is he's shooting. Please, let me get it straight. I don't want to die."

"John Phillip Walker, 573137, 26 March 1938."

"So you have been lying. Why will you not tell me your rank? Did you steal that uniform? What...is...your...rank?"

"It's Lieutenant; Lieutenant Jack Walk... Lieutenant John Phillip Walker, United States Navy, 573137, 26 March 1938."

"Ooooooh, you have made a mistake, Lieutenant. The Geneva Convention does not require you to give your branch of service. I know that you are in the navy, of course, but you must be more careful. How can I practice my tricks as an interrogator if you insist on giving me too much information at once?"

Jack's head was hurting and he was getting woozy again. He knew that he was making mistakes, but what the hell difference did all this make? How the hell is someone supposed to live up to the Geneva Convention rules, the Code of Conduct and all the other bullshit those rear echelon generals and the bastards in striped pants dream up? "This is the real thing and I can't even get my name straight without getting chewed up."

A prisoner of war is in a tight spot right from the start. He is a military man supposedly protected by a set of rules of war agreed to by most of the nations of the world. Right there is the oxymoron of all times. We make up rules about the civilized way to kill, maim, and destroy. Urbane gentlemen sit down at polished tables and sip tea while discussing what is a fair way for men to kill each other. Once armies clash and the slaughter begins, there will probably be prisoners taken. There always have been. Centuries before, prisoners became slaves or they were used for target practice, or whatever the conquerors decided. Now we have rules. The fly in the diplomatic ointment is that several nations didn't make it to the party in Geneva. It's like sitting down to play bridge and finding that your opponents plan to use meat axes rather than a deck of cards.

Jack had thought about these anomalies many times before. They had been the topic of discussion many times during those famous bull sessions back at the base. What happens when you become a prisoner of war by a nation that your country doesn't even recognize officially? There are no rules except the ones dreamed up in some Pentagon think tank by patriotic zealots. An American fighting man must resist interrogation. He must attempt to escape. He must join with his fellow prisoners to form a chain of command within the ranks of the prisoners. He must accept no favors from the enemy, nor must he give assistance to the enemy. Even under torture or threat of death he must resist his captors' attempts to subvert his thinking. In other words, a prisoner who may be sick, wounded, hungry, thirsty, dirty, friendless, scared shitless, and at the mercy of god knows what kind of maniac must remain a model

American fighting man. If he signs a piece of paper or admits to lies about his country for the sake of a little sleep or relief from pain, he might later face a court martial -- provided he lives. All the while he knows full well that other Americans are refusing induction into the armed forces, shouting out their hate for the government and all it stands for, and vilifying the American fighting men. There are Americans sending gifts of money and medicine to the enemy. There are Americans visiting the enemy and returning home to tell the rest of the country the enemy side of the story. They accuse Americans fighting in Viet Nam of being bloodthirsty, baby-killing rapists; mercenaries destroying a small nation of peasants for the ambitions of the rich industrialists. They say the United States is keeping the war going so America can ravage Viet Nam and steal her wealth and enslave her people.

These thoughts raced through Jack's mind as he tried to comprehend what was happening to him. No one even knew where he was or what was happening to him, but he was supposed to stick to the Code. The hand placed gently on his cheek brought him back to the mud hut and the smiling face before him.

"Lieutenant, you are not paying attention to me. Please now, try to cooperate. Give me your name, rank, service number, and date of birth. That is all I want from you. Nothing more. Just what the Geneva Convention says you are supposed to give to me."

"Lieutenant John Phillip Walker. 573137. 26 March 1938."

"Thank you, Lieutenant. Your superiors will be proud of you. They are probably sitting down for their afternoon cocktails right now and saying 'That young Lieutenant Walker is a fine military man.' Can you not see them in their starched uniforms? Lounging there in Saigon. No problems, no worries. They never have to go out and face our soldiers in battle. All they have to do is ensure that there are enough men like you to go on to the front lines and fight; brave men who will face the enemy and die if necessary to preserve the precious system. They will be proud of you.

"And what about your wife, Lieutenant? Will she be proud of you? You are married, are you not, Lieutenant? Certainly you are. You wear the ring to prove it. Yes. Is she pretty? Of course she would be. I am sure you would rather talk about her than those starched shirts back in Saigon. Talking about your wife certainly can not be breaking the rules can it, Lieutenant?"

This was the hard part, sitting and listening. Name, rank, and service number. Don't even think anything else. Don't listen to this guy. One word from you and he will have you in front of a firing squad as a war criminal.

"I suppose you did not hear me, Lieutenant. I asked if your wife was pretty. Is she one of those tall, good looking American girls? Long blond hair? Pretty teeth? Tell me about her, Lieutenant. Do you miss her?"

"Screw you," Jack thought to himself. "You're not going to get me to talk to you. I'll think about other things. Not my wife, or baby, or Timber Cove or anything about home. I'll think about my job, and escaping, the crew that was lost. But I won't talk to you."

"You are almost smiling, Lieutenant. I guess I was right. Your wife is pretty, is she not? But you do not have to worry. Someone will be looking after her. Is it not right that your navy sends an officer to visit your wife if you are missing? Don't they send someone to look after her, hold her hand, and dry her tears."

Jack was struggling with himself. The dirty, evil grin on the interrogator's face was getting to him. What right did this son of a bitch have even talking about Sally? No, don't get mad. Don't even think. Just play stupid. Don't even think. Don't think.

"Yes, Lieutenant. Someone is looking after her. Some stateside officer sitting there, right in your house. Sitting by your wife and patting her on the knee, telling her not to worry. Does your wife have pretty legs, Lieutenant? Do you think that she will mind when that officer puts his hand on her leg?"

"This is too much. I could break this little bastard in half before anyone knew what was happening," thought Jack. The rage inside him was getting to be more than he could suppress.

"Come on, Lieutenant, we're friends. Tell me about her legs. Are they long and slim? Are they soft? Do you think that stateside officer will have much trouble getting in between them? What do you think, Lieu...?"

"Shut up." Jack screamed the words out as he lunged at the little man. He threw his whole weight behind the fist as he tried to smash the grinning face that taunted him. But he missed. The little man stepped aside easily and smashed a fist into Jack's kidney. Jack screamed again as he was kicked hard in the stomach and then in the groin. He felt his stomach churning and he wanted to vomit. His groin was searing and Jack lay there praying that he wouldn't be hit again.

The interrogator took hold of Jack's head firmly in both hands and held his face close to Jack's. The smile was gone. The face was passive now, almost blank with maybe a touch of a smile of satisfaction around the eyes. The voice was soft. "I could kill you now, Lieutenant. But I will not. We have much to talk about. Your superiors in Saigon sipping their cocktails. Your pretty wife and her pretty legs. Before I am through with you, Lieutenant, you will be offering me those legs." And then he slammed his knee into Jack's face and watched him sag to the floor, bloody and degraded. The punches and kicks had hurt badly, but the little man knew that the words had hurt more. He had discovered the crack in the armor. This one had been child's play. It was usually easier to break a man down when he was alone. It had been more difficult back at the prison in Hanoi. The prisoners had managed to establish a network and support each other. Breaking the prisoners' morale was the first order of business. And if the interrogators could get the prisoners working against each other, all the better. Jack's antagonist really didn't want anything from him. It was all part of a game he liked to play.

As the interrogator went out, the guard slipped in and left a bowl of food. The flies and ants would probably finish it before Jack recovered enough to even know it was there.

CHAPTER 7

"Mrs. Walker? Mrs. John Walker?" The pleasant voice sounded like an old friend.

"Yes, this is Mrs. Walker. Who is calling please?"

"Sorry to hear about your husband, Mrs. Walker. He's evidently in a pretty bad jam." The voice was still pleasant, but Sally didn't like the tone.

"Who is this calling, please; do I know you?"

"No, Mrs. Walker. You don't know me. But I know who you are and I feel sorry for you. I feel sorry for a woman who has to carry the child of a killer. That's what your husband is and he's going to get what he has coming to him...."

Sally slammed down the receiver. Dear Lord, she thought, as she sank to the floor sobbing. The choking sobs tore at her. Then the phone rang again. "Leave me alone, go away!" She almost couldn't get the words out. "Don't, please don't tell me those things." She fumbled the phone back into the cradle and struggled into the bathroom. She was sick to her stomach and thought she was going to throw up. Sally tried to calm herself, but as she sat on the edge of the tub she felt something was wrong. She saw blood was staining her maternity slacks. "Help, help! The baby, the baby!"

Up until today, things had been going well. Sally had called on her inner strength to get herself under control after the news came about Jack. Others had tried to help her, but since she had moved up to the suburbs east of the San Francisco Bay Area after Jack went overseas, she hadn't gotten reestablished with the few people she had known before. She had to do it all herself. She had to keep the apartment running normally, and give Todd a stable home. She had to do it. No one could help, especially during the long, painful nights when she lay alone in the big bed. But this bolt from the blue wasn't fair. The hateful phone call; that awful, syrupy voice, that horrible voice.

She struggled back out to the telephone and called her neighbor, an older woman who was usually home. They hadn't gotten to be close friends, but the woman seemed nice, and like Sally, guarded her privacy. The neighbor picked up the phone on the third ring. "This is your neighbor, Sally Walker. I need help. Can you come over?"

There was a knock at the door before Sally hung up the phone. Her neighbor was there to help. "What's wrong? The baby?" She saw the blood and how Sally was hunched over in pain and immediately summed up the situation. "Sit down and I'll call an ambulance. Where is the little boy? Do I need to do anything for him?"

Sally was so grateful she started to cry. Thank God this woman is the take-charge type. "Todd is fine. He's in his room. I don't need an ambulance. I could go in a cab."

"You will do no such thing. The navy got you into this mess; the least they can do is take care of you properly. My husband was in the army so I know how to work the system. Just sit there and I'll get things going."

It took the ambulance almost fifteen minutes to arrive. Sally got to know her neighbor during those minutes. Todd would be just fine and if she had to stay at the hospital overnight the woman said that she would bring a blanket and sleep on the couch so Todd could at least have the comfort of his own room.

The ambulance attendants did some routine tests on the spot and called the hospital for permission to give Sally a sedative. She was feeling quite relaxed by the time she got to the ambulance. There was a whir of activity that passed beyond Sally's cognizance as she rode to the hospital. She woke up in bed with a nurse at her side.

"We gave you a sedative. You're fine and so is the baby. Your neighbors are looking after your little boy. I'm your nurse. The doctor will be back in a few minutes."

"What happened? How did I get here?"

"I'm not sure. You arrived by ambulance. Can't you remember what happened?"

"Vaguely. I had a phone call. A horrible call." Sally started to shake. The nurse put a cold towel on her forehead and stroked her hair gently.

"Here's the doctor now. She said she got a phone call, doctor. It must have been something awful."

The doctor came in and smiled at Sally. "What can you remember about what set this off? Not your husband, is it?" He went about checking pulse and heartbeat. The doctor was young, but kindly and seemed to be genuinely interested in Sally's problem.

"Some horrible person called me and said terrible things about Jack, my husband, and about how my baby would....Doctor, my baby, have I lost the baby? Tell me what's happening. I can't lose the baby. It's Jack's baby. Help me."

"Now take it easy, Sally, there's no problem with the baby. You're both fine. You have to relax. Whoever phoned you can't reach you here. But I think this is a coincidence. I don't want you to associate the phone call with your reaction. You had some cramps and there might be some minor infection, but you're fine. You have nothing to worry about. I'm going to give you a stronger sedative. You need to rest and build up your strength. Your baby is fine, now go to sleep."

"Wait, please. My son, Todd. Where is he?"

The doctor explained that Todd was fine and that the neighbor was looking after him. It all came back to Sally and she relaxed. The doctor's order to relax was just what Sally needed. It helped to have someone taking care of her for a change. She took the pills the doctor prescribed and nodded off immediately.

The next morning Sally was feeling better. She could talk about the phone call and she remembered the officer who had come to visit her. She wondered if she should tell him; after all, what could he do?

The only thing to do would be to change the phone to an unlisted number. No, what if Jack tried to call? He might. How would he get in touch with her? What if the Navy had word. They wouldn't be able to get in touch with her. Her mind was reeling. Calm down and think, girl. Yes, tell the Commander. He could inform the Navy. Oh, God, what if they are trying to get me right now? "Nurse, nurse! Where is that damned button? Nurse!"

A young girl in a candy-striped uniform hurried into the room. She was a pretty girl and Sally could see that she was doing her best to put on her official look. "Yes, Mrs. Walker, what can I do for you?"

"Where's my purse. I have to make a phone call. Where is the phone? It's terribly important. I have to phone."

"Please calm down, Mrs. Walker. Here's your purse. There's a phone down the hall. Let me get a wheel chair for you. I'll take you down. No, please, don't try to get up. Please!"

The official look was gone. The poor girl was frightened to death that Sally would try to get up against the doctor's orders, and she would be to blame. Sally sensed the young girl's feeling of panic and saw it in her eyes. "All right, I won't get up, but please hurry."

The young hospital volunteer gave Sally a big, bright, thankful smile and rushed out the door. She was back almost immediately with an immense old wooden wheelchair, something that had obviously weathered several wars. For all the latest techniques and equipment in military hospitals they managed to hang on to the past in the form of patient comfort items.

The young girl helped Sally into the chair. Sally felt fine. She could have easily walked down to the phone but orders were orders and there wasn't any use trying to change the rules. The "doctor-gods" had evidently left word that Sally was not to get up. What do they do with young volunteers who violate the eleventh commandment? -- *The doctor's word is law.* It must be something horrible to have the poor girl so frightened.

Sally phoned Lieutenant Commander Karpaski. She told him about the call and where she was. He assured her that he would be right over and he insisted on stopping by the apartment to check on young Todd before coming to the hospital.

"I couldn't help overhearing, Mrs. Walker. I ... I know how you must feel." The young girl broke into tears and suddenly Sally was the nurse. She started to get up, but the young girl put her hands on Sally's shoulders and held her down. "I'm fine. It's just that I know how you must feel."

"How could you know?" thought Sally. "What does young girl like you know about anything?" She was about to say something to stop the flow of sympathy, but the girl's face held a look of pain that stopped her. "Are you married?"

"No, it's my brother. He's missing too. They think he might be alive, but we haven't heard anything. I'm sorry, Mrs. Walker. I didn't mean to break down. You've got enough trouble without mine being added on."

"Yes, well don't worry about breaking down. I've been doing my share of that this past week."

"The past week?" Your husband has been missing a week? I mean, that's how long ago we heard about my brother."

"Well, we have something in common, young lady. How about getting me back to my room and we'll both have a good cry."

Susie Dunlay was still puttering around Sally's room doing all kinds of things that didn't need doing when Lieutenant Commander Karpaski came in. "I guess I had better go," said Susie.

"If you have time, give me a call at home. I'll introduce you to Todd. He's only two, but he has an eye for the pretty girls."

"I'd like that, Mrs. Walker. I really would. I'll call you soon." Then she turned to Lieutenant Commander Karpaski. "Please don't stay too long. The doctor wants Mrs. Walker to rest today." And with her official look firmly in place, Susie left the room.

"I've contacted the FBI, Mrs. Walker. They have a special team that works with the phone company on these things. Oh, before I forget; I went by to check on your son. He's getting along fine. Just one thing, what is a num gaw?"

"Did he call you a num gaw? That's a special word he uses only for very special people. I'm not sure exactly what it means but it goes along with the blue uniform. When I find out whether it's good or bad, I'll let you know."

"Yes, I'll be interested to know if I'm a good num gaw or a bad one. Well, back to business. Inspector Delcarthy will drop in on you, as soon as you feel up to it, and arrange to have your phone line monitored -- that is if you will consent to a phone tap. It's the only way they can help."

"Good grief, Commander, of course I'll consent. You've been reading too many congressional investigation stories. If it will help catch that horrible person they can tap and monitor as much as they want."

"They have to be careful. You'll have to sign a waiver and all that. I'll check with your doctor and arrange to have Mr. Delcarthy drop by your house as soon as you get home. And don't worry, they'll stop the calls." He muttered something under his breath about "damned cowards" and then he smiled and said "Goodbye, Mrs. Walker. Hope you're feeling better soon." Then he left.

Susie Dunlay was back in the room before the door had a chance to close. She had flowers and clean sheets with her and Sally got the V.I.P. treatment for the rest of the day.

CHAPTER 8

Jeff had been listening quietly for several minutes. The voices sounded normal and unhurried. He couldn't tell what they were doing, but it didn't sound like they were searching for him. Besides they seemed to have come from the opposite direction from where he had been. After he had awakened, two more had come up the trail and they had come from toward the sea. If he could only see them, they could be friendly, and he could tell that they had food. Jeff was hungry. It had been some time since he had had anything to eat. He decided to at least try to take a look. He moved slowly, an inch at a time literally. Then he froze. The voices sounded excited. "Oh, dear God, they've seen me." Jeff didn't move a muscle. A little bug landed in his ear and buzzed and flew around until he wanted to tear his ear off, but he forced himself to remain motionless. Then the voices started to move up the trail from where he had come. At the same time the little bug freed itself and flew off.

Jeff slumped and laid there, his heart pounding so hard against his chest that he thought he was having a heart attack. He closed his eyes and took a few deep breaths to calm himself. Those brief moments aged him ten years. He waited until he was sure the voices were gone, and then he crept out of his hiding place. Maybe they left some food, just a scrap. But there was nothing. "Chintzy bastards," he thought. "Not even a grain of rice." He looked up and down the path but he could only see about fifty feet in either direction. "This is no good. I could walk right into a patrol and then what the hell would I do? Say howdy, and hope they mistook me for another gook?" It was a painful decision, but the only thing to do. Jeff moved back into the jungle and resumed his slow trek to the sea, one foot at a time.

The jungle offers a bountiful harvest if you know where to look. Fruit on the trees, edible roots, even the little things that crawled around would sustain life if you had the guts to eat them. Jeff found a few odds and ends to nibble on and water was available in stumps and in leaves here and there. "Take it slow. No need to hurry now.'" Jeff told himself. "Keep heading for the ocean. No need to rush. Stay off the trails." It had been dumb luck that morning that he had decided to get off the trail and rest or he would have walked right into that bunch, whoever they were. Jeff fought his way through the underbrush for four days. He fell in his tracks when he was too tired to go any further, and when he woke he started to crawl again. After the second day, he moved mostly on his hands and knees. His foot started to hurt. He could feel it swelling inside his boot. But he made the pain work for him. He was scratched and cut from the bushes and thorns. His hands and face were lumpy from insect bites and his groin was a raw, red blister from heat rash. Time and again he wanted to just lay down and die, and more than once he gave in to the impulse. But then his aching foot would waken him and he got up and pushed a little further. It was tougher to get up and move after each time he fell asleep. Just a short nap, a little rest was all he wanted.

He was about to give in again when he heard the staccato thumping of a helicopter. It was circling in his vicinity. Jeff got to his feet and for the first time in three days he looked up at the sky or where the sky should be. The green roof of the jungle covered him. Then, through the roof, he saw the chopper, a big beautiful chopper. He waved his arms and tried to yell but his voice came out in a pathetic little squeak. He was saved. He was going to get out of this hellhole. They were looking for him. But the chopper flew away. Jeff stared up at the empty sky. He looked like some kind of broken puppet standing there in the jungle, a ragged, dirty, doll of a man.

His arms moved in a slow, disjointed way and then his knees bumped together and he slowly slumped to the ground. His two-week growth of beard was filthy and matted with bugs and leaves and dirt. His eyes were sunken back into their sockets. The once handsome, clean-shaven face was a rotted death mask. He crumpled a bit at a time. He made strange grunting noises, like a sick animal. He was going to die in this God-forsaken green sweatbox. He was going to die. That noise, like the beat of wings. Didn't death ride on huge wings? Death was coming. What did death do? Swoop in and rip out the soul? Leave the body; the dirty, torn ragged, crumpled body? He wasn't afraid. Death couldn't be any worse than the hell of the past two weeks. Get ready. Get ready. Here comes death. How do you get ready?

"Our father, who art in heaven. In heaven? How could anyone in heaven know about this place? This is hell. Death already came. I'm in hell. There is no heaven."

Jeff didn't even know what he was doing, but he was crawling. The habit of the past days had started him crawling again. His mind was full of strange shapes and colors. It was like he was outside his body watching himself crawl. "So this is Hell." You crawl through a jungle forever. You can't even lie down and die. You crawl and make strange noises and watch the shapes and colors. At least it didn't hurt. Maybe Hell wasn't so bad. The wings are still there. They're beating and thundering. Why doesn't death come down and take him? "Aren't I even worth taking? There, there it comes, like a fresh breeze. Here comes death now. You can feel the wind from the wings. It's cooler. And there are voices. Must be angels -- or devils. It's cool now. Maybe this won't be so bad after all." Then the nightmares came. Voices, pain, more voices in the distance. Now and then there was a face. and the pain, and the shapes and colors. Always the damned shapes and colors. And pain.

"What do you think, doctor, is he going to make it?"

"Well, if being completely dehydrated from diarrhea, being on the verge of gangrene in his leg, being half eaten by bugs, totally exhausted and nearly starved doesn't bother him too much, he has a pretty good chance. Jesus, he must be a tough mother to keep going like he did."

It was three days before Jeff came out of his delirium. He woke up in the middle of the night in the dim light of the hospital. He was sure he was dead. There was a needle in his arm leading to a tube that led to a bottle suspended over his bed. "What's that? They're embalming me." He tried to scream but he had no voice. He tried to move but he was too weak. The nurse came to him immediately.

"Can you hear me?" Her voice was quiet. Her cool hand on his forehead was like a gentle breeze. "Can you hear me?"

Jeff couldn't answer. He tried to nod his head, but it barely moved.

"If you can hear me, just listen. You're okay. You're in a hospital and you're going to be okay."

The words didn't mean much to Jeff. He felt himself relax and the awful aching and the terror of the past week subsided. Nothing seemed real. The Lieutenant back in the jungle didn't even enter his head. He opened his eyes briefly and stared blankly at the nurse. Then he fell back asleep.

CHAPTER 9

"Hello, Mrs. Walker, this is Susan Dunlay. You said to call you some time and we could visit."

"Fine" Sally answered "but if you and I are going to be friends, you're going to have to call me Sally. I'm here every day. When can you come over?"

"How would tomorrow afternoon be?"

"Fine, in fact, why don't you plan to stay the night? We could cook up a nice dinner and spend the evening." Sally had gotten to like young Susie during the two days she had spent in the hospital. And the thought of having someone to talk to who wouldn't be on guard every minute, afraid to mention Jack, was a relieving thought.

"Wonderful. I'd love to stay the night. Can I bring anything?"

"Just yourself and a lot of energy. I'm going to turn Todd loose on you."

After the call, Susie went out to the kitchen where her mother was fixing dinner. "Remember the woman I told you about at the hospital, the one whose husband was missing about the same time as Jeff? She asked me to come over tomorrow and spend the night. Will it be all right?"

Mrs. Dunlay didn't even look up from her work. "Suit yourself. No one around here cares what I think."

"Mother, I care. We all care."

"You don't care." Mrs. Dunlay turned on her daughter and screamed the words out. "You don't care. Your father doesn't care. My son murdered in some strange country and you all act like nothing has happened. You don't care."

Susie called to her mother as Mrs. Dunlay ran out of the kitchen, crying, but she knew it was no use trying to reason with her. Anita Dunlay had gotten worse this past week. She hadn't spoken to her husband, and when anyone tried to talk to her she started crying and ran from the room. Susie didn't take it personally, but she did wish that her mother would let her talk about Jeff.

Susie started to take over the cooking chore that her mother had abruptly left behind when her brother Les came into the kitchen and asked, "Did I hear the grand dame in her crying act again?"

Susie glared at her brother. "You stupid little toad. The more I think about it the more I think this whole thing is your fault. You and your communist friends."

"Ho, ho, big sister. Just because I have the guts to stand up and say what I think about this war doesn't make me a communist."

"I didn't say you were a communist. You're too stupid to be one. You're a stupid little boy trying to act like a man. You're jealous of your brother and you're spoiled rotten. And if I hear you call mother a 'Grand Dame' again, I'll rip you dirty little tongue out."

"Oh, can it, you dumb bitch."

Susie picked up the cookbook that was open on the table and heaved it at him with all her strength. The edge of the heavy book caught Les on the forehead and stunned him. He slumped back against the refrigerator with a wide-eyed look of amazement. He heard his sister call him a "stupid little toad" again as she marched out of the kitchen.

★ ★ ★

Jeff had been waking up on and off for two more days after the nurse first talked to him. He had been eating a little bit and was starting to get some strength back. But none of the conversations made sense. People kept asking him who he was and then floating away. Jeff had thought to himself that this was some kind of trick.

If these were really Americans they would know who he was. The lieutenant flashed back into his mind a couple of times and before he could put the whole picture together, he passed out again. About the fourth day in the hospital Jeff started coming out of the fog.

He had been awake for about two hours and the puzzle was going together nicely now. It had been dark when he woke up and the ward was quiet. He realized where he was and an enormous relief came over him. He was in an American hospital. He was safe. He lay quietly and tried to remember everything that had happened. He remembered the lieutenant and the day that he had been captured. He remembered the escape, and everything up to the time he left the trail was coming clear, but he had no idea how he had gotten to the hospital.

About 0600 a nurse came around and saw that Jeff was awake. She didn't say anything, just rested a cool hand on his forehead and smiled.

"Thanks, nurse. That feels good."

"You're looking better, young man. Feel like talking?"

"I feel more like eating." And for the second time since he had started running to locate the mortars outside the village, Jeff smiled.

"I'll have something brought over right away. Try to stay with us this time."

Jeff had been thinking steak and eggs, but wiser heads prevailed and he had to settle for tea and toast and some juice. Shortly after Jeff finished breakfast a marine captain and two sergeants came into the ward. They talked with the nurse and a man that Jeff assumed was the doctor for a few minutes and then they came over to his bed."

"Feel up to some questions this morning?"

"Yes, sir."

"Good. Let's start at the beginning. Who are you and what were you doing out there on the beach where they found you?"

"Corporal Geoffrey Dunlay, United States Marine Corps, sir. I was on ops with the second battalion when we got hit; I guess it was a couple of weeks ago. I hurt my foot and was taken prisoner. I don't know what happened to my platoon. They were taking a real pasting when I got hit."

The captain looked at Jeff. "Hit? Were you shot too? The doctor didn't say anything about that. Just the punji stake."

"I remember having a hell of a sore rib. My flak jacket must have stopped the bullet or whatever it was that knocked me out. It happened about the same time I stepped on the stake."

"That makes sense. Go on. What else can you remember?"

Jeff recounted what he could remember about his capture and the trek to the hamlet and the hut he was confined in. "A couple of days after they took me, they brought in a navy lieutenant. We were together for a couple of days before I got away." Jeff got nervous. He wasn't sure what to say. The sight of the captain and the two sergeants brought back the boot camp lectures and the drill instructor's admonishments that marines never leave their dead or wounded behind. Everyone comes out together or no one comes out. How was he going to explain that he left without the lieutenant?

"Just the two of you, corporal?"

"Yes, sir. I don't know how long ago and I don't know where you found me. But I spent quite a few days trying to get to the coast from where they had us."

Even before Jeff had finished the sentence, one of the sergeants was on his way out the door. Jeff wasn't sure why, but the thought of the sergeant rounding up a firing squad flashed through his mind. He blurted out "I didn't want to leave the lieutenant. I couldn't wake him up. He was hurt."

"Easy, corporal. It looks like you did one hell of a job just getting yourself free. We'll get to the lieutenant in a few minutes. The sergeant went to check the intelligence sheets on MIAs. Maybe we can piece this together and help locate him."

Jeff felt a rush of relief at the captain's words. He gave him his service number and organization and all the details that he could remember. Before he had finished, the second sergeant left with a book full of notes to check out. They had spent about an hour with questions and answers, but Jeff was obviously tiring and he started to slip away. The doctor came over and insisted that the interrogation end. Jeff wanted to go on because he knew that there was a chance to save the lieutenant if he could give them enough information.

Finally a compromise was reached. "Give him a few hours to rest" the doctor said "and we'll try to get some more solid food in him later. I promise you, captain, it will be faster my way."

"Right, Doc. You're right. But this man's outfit and several others have run into large-scale resistance in the past three weeks and in every case the VC took prisoners. Corporal Dunlay is the first man we've gotten back. We've got to know why all this attention to getting prisoners, and where they're taking them. From what the corporal said, they could have just left him and he might have died. We have to know what this is all about.

★ ★ ★

Jack Walker was living a nightmare twenty-four hours a day since Jeff had escaped. He was pretty much recovered physically from the beating he had taken from the interrogator, but it was taking every ounce of his will to keep from going out of his mind. After the beating, he had been left alone in the dark for about three days. Food and water had been slipped into the hut while he was sleeping. He never saw anyone. On the third day the interrogator came back. He had two guards with him and they brought two stools. The stools were set down close together and Jack was put on one of them. The interrogator sat on the other stool smoking a cigarette and doing nothing except looking at Jack, sometimes smiling. The two guards just stood there. Every once in a while it looked like the interrogator was going to say something, but then he would break off, take a puff from his cigarette, and continue staring. After a while, maybe a half an hour, the interrogator and the two guards walked out. Jack thought for a moment that he was going to have the luxury of the stools to sit on in the mud-floored hut, but they were just teasing him. The door flew open again and the guards came in laughing and took the stools out.

Jack was alone again for a few hours and then it started. Every fifteen minutes the door opened. If Jack was lying down they prodded him and made him stand up. If he was asleep they flashed a light in his face. No one said anything to him. They just forced him to his feet and once he was upright, they left. Jack had no idea how long this had gone on. But he was reasonably sure it was for more than a day, perhaps two days. Then it stopped. For almost four hours he was left alone. He tried to sleep but every noise grated on his nerves and he kept waking up. At no time was he fully asleep or fully awake. The procedure was destroying his will to resist. Even his will to live.

The door opened again and three guards came in with the two stools and this time they brought a table. Jeff was put on one of the stools at the table and one of the guards took the other stool across from him. A piece of paper was placed before him and a pen was placed in his hand. The writing on the paper was in Vietnamese except for his name under the line at the bottom. The guard across the table pointed at the paper and said "Sign". Jack looked at him, trying to remain as bland as possible. The guard kept saying "Sign, you sign, sign." and stabbing at the paper with his finger.

Jack kept looking at him. He laid the pen down and one of the guards picked it up and forced it back into his hand. Then he threw the pen on the floor. The guard picked it up and forced it into his hand again. All the time the other guard kept saying "Sign, you sign". Then as quickly as it had started, the guards took the stools and table and left the hut.

Jack knew what they were doing. They wanted him to sign a confession or something. All the harassing for the past days had been to weaken him and get him to admit his guilt. Jack thought of Sally and said a short prayer. The pity he had felt for himself so often lately came over him. He fought it. His only job now was to keep from cracking. They weren't beating him or torturing him, it was all mental. He had to remember that and keep reminding himself.

He started to doze off and the door opened. Just that. A door opening and he was ready to scream. His nerves were shot. He fought down the impulse to rage out at his captors. Why wouldn't they leave him alone? What the hell good would a confession written in Vietnamese be to them anyway? But here they were again with the stools and the table. He was dragged roughly off the floor and placed on his stool. It was almost impossible for him to keep his eyes open. He was desperate for sleep. The guards prodded him with their rifles every time his eyes closed. One of them grabbed his hair and pulled it back until he thought it was coming out by the roots. For what seemed like hours they kept him awake, sitting on that little stool. His mind was a jumble. The guard at the table would jab at the paper and say "Sign". Jack realized that he had been wrong before. This damned well was physical torture.

The interrogator came in. Jack wanted to cry and scream and pass out all at the same time. The sight of that face that he had come to hate gave him some strength.

"Your signature, Lieutenant. Then we will leave you alone." He motioned to the guard who took the pen and placed it in Jack's hand and moved his hand over to the paper where he was to sign. Jack used his last bit of energy to break the pen and throw the pieces on the floor. The guards moved toward him with their rifles raised but the interrogator waived them away.

"Why will you not sign? It is only an acknowledgment that you are in our custody and that you are well."

Jack glared at the smiling face.

"We need to have this to send to the Red Cross. Do you not want your wife to know where you are? Oh, I see. You think this is some sort of a confession as in the movies they showed you. No, Lieutenant, it is just a statement that all prisoners of war must sign. It says that you have been captured and that you are well. We send this to the Red Cross and then they can forward mail and packages from your wife. That is all it is. Now please sign the paper and we will end this nonsense."

* * *

"Sally and Susie. It sounds like a vaudeville act. We could work up a song and dance routine. That would give us something to do while we wait for this stupid war to end. The way it has been going we could win the Guiness World Record for vaudeville acts. This goddamn war is going to go on forever. How I hate it. Damn, damn, damn!" Tears came to Sally's eyes as she ranted about the war, but she was relieved to have someone to talk to that understood.

Susie wasn't saying much because she had her family to talk things over with. With her mother on the edge of a breakdown, her father lost in another generation, and her brother acting like a total ass it wasn't much help, but at least she had some opportunity to talk about Jeff with people who loved him and were in the same boat with her.

Sally was pretty much alone. Her father had left the family when she was a little girl and her mother had died five years ago. It was one of the major circumstances that she and Jack shared. She didn't have much contact with the rest of her family, the aunts, uncles and cousins. Being an only child there were no brothers or sisters to call up and talk to. Normally it didn't bother her. She was happy not to have to cater to a bunch of relatives. But the last few weeks she had been paying a toll. All her feelings had been bottled up because no one understood. Even Lieutenant Commander Karpaski didn't understand. Especially Karpaski. One day when they had been talking he mentioned that he was waiting for orders to Viet Nam. He felt it was his duty to volunteer. Some stupid male thing about getting in the war. Men felt that way. Military men were impossible. They needed that bravado bullshit to justify their existence. How could any sane person talk about wanting to go to war? They put it in terms of doing one's duty, or following orders, or making all their training pay off. Whatever they called it, it was bullshit.

Sally wondered if she was going to corrupt Susie with her language. She never was one to mince words. "Susie, I'm sorry. I hope you don't think I'm a fallen woman. Sometimes I have to say what's inside and it comes out less than ladylike."

"You know I'm shocked. My image of the perfect navy wife has been shattered."

They both had a good laugh. Sally knew it was a stupid thing to say the minute the words left her mouth. It was so good to have someone around who would accept her as she was. It had taken a while to get Jack broken into her freewheeling style of speech but he was so in love with her that she could have grown a tail and horns and it would have been fine with him. It took a bit longer to break down the stiff-necked senior officers' wives, not to mention the senior officers. But eventually almost everyone in the navy family circle got to know Sally and if they didn't approve of or accept her style, they put up with it.

Sally was smart, she was sophisticated, and she was independent. She could get away with swearing like a fo'c'le seaman on occasion. Not many could and those that could were usually men, rarely women. She tried to keep it under control, but sometimes she just let loose. Soon after she and Jack were married they were invited to call on the commanding officer for cocktails and the traditional get acquainted meeting. When they arrived they were met by the commanding officer and his wife and introduced to the visiting admiral and his chief of staff. Jack's executive officer was there too. And the officers' wives were there. Wives were always an afterthought, a fact of military life that always galled Sally. Jack had warned her before they went that things might be a bit formal and he had begged her to be on her good behavior. Jack was in his dress blues and Sally wore hat and gloves and her primmest suit. They could have been going to visit the Pope. And sure enough, it was formal and polite. The admiral told a few polite sea stories and a decorous joke. Everyone laughed politely at the proper time and congratulated the admiral. Then the Captain told a story and everyone laughed and congratulated the Captain. Jack and Sally were asked polite questions about how they like married life and the navy.

A second round of drinks were served, then a third. The admiral told another story. This time he was better lubricated and the joke less polite, and everyone really laughed. While they were laughing, Sally blurted out "Admiral, you old son of a bitch, you really do have a sense of humor."

The executive officer, who hadn't said a word all evening, was just biting into his martini olive. He almost choked and in reaction spit the olive out with some force. It flew across the room and landed down the front of the admiral's wife's dress. No one was sure what to do. The exec asked if there was some way he could be of assistance. Mrs. Admiral's reply was somewhat slurred, but it became obvious that Sally wasn't the only one who could turn a phrase when she told the exec that there was no way he could help unless he wanted his ass in a sling.

The ice had been broken. The whole damned dam had burst. It turned out to be the best "navy" party Jack and Sally ever went to. And Sally knew from that moment on that there was nothing for a navy wife to fear from those blue suited martinets with all their ribbons and medals. They took their pants off one leg at a time just like everyone else. And their wives were a bit more human than one might think at first glance. Even so it was a long time before any of the senior people acknowledged what a good time they had at the captain's party. It was a non-event; and even though Sally knew what they were really like, the senior wives didn't let her forget her place. They clucked and looked shocked when she swore. One of them even tried to take her aside and give her a lesson in etiquette at a party one night. No one was ever sure exactly what went on in the ladies' room that evening, but the two never spoke to one another again and their mutual dislike was legend in the little circle. Thank God for transfers.

Sally told Susie the story about the party and went on to tell her about life as a navy wife; the transfers, the loneliness, the good times, the excitement, the people. She wondered if Jack was thinking about the days they were first married and going to parties and generally enjoying life. She wondered if Jack was still alive. How could he not be? He was part of her life. Her thoughts were intertwined with his. He was a living part of her and her son and the baby that was coming.

★ ★ ★

Jack had not signed the paper that the interrogator kept pushing at him. After a while it became a deadly game of who would give in first. Jack had no illusions about the outcome. He would lose one way or another. He was numb from lack of sleep and his body hurt from the beating he had taken. He was suffering from a horrible depression. Why had the world forsaken him to these people who were treating him like an animal? He was on the verge of giving up. He was going to sign the damned paper and get it over with.

Who gave a shit anyway? He wasn't proving anything to anyone. He would be killed eventually and no one would ever know what took place in this grass hut in this goddamned jungle in this asshole of a place. But he couldn't even get his mind to work fast enough to give up.

The session abruptly ended and he was alone again. He was given some food and water and allowed to sleep. It wasn't the deep sleep of someone who had been awake for a long time. The interrogator had done his job well. The least noise brought awakening and terror, and fear of torture. Except for being pushed around and hit a few times he hadn't been too badly abused, physically. But the interrogator had talked about what they could do to him. He had planted the seed. From time to time the door opened and someone would look in, but the sessions seemed to be over.

Jack had no idea how long he had slept. Actually it was about five hours. He woke up and lay quietly for a long time. At first he couldn't remember where he was. There was a feeling of dread, but he couldn't place the source. The hut was dark. It was quiet outside. Slowly it came back to him. The nightmare. Was he asleep or dreaming? Was he really a prisoner? As the fog cleared inside his head he began to take inventory. He let out a low moan and realized that he could hear. Then he moved his arms and touched his face. He had all his fingers and his face seemed in one piece. He sat up slowly and felt his legs. They were both there. His testicles. What about his testicles? That was what the interrogator had threatened him with. He said that a man whose wife was with other men, and she was surely with other men by now, a man like that did not need testicles. He ran his hand down inside his trousers and felt his penis and testicles. They hadn't cut anything off. Jack giggled to himself. Then he started to stroke himself. In no time he had an erection and he felt the thrill of it. His mind raced through a dozen girls he had known and all their features blended into a composite.

Amid all the pain and tiredness the thought of sex was a welcomed relief. The door flew open and two soldiers came in laughing and pointing at him. Jack felt a rush of embarrassment and then dread came over him again. The pleasant thoughts disappeared.

The soldiers stopped laughing and prodded him to his feet with their rifles. All thought of the momentary ecstasy was gone now. He was pushed outside. A small band of soldiers were standing near the edge of the clearing. They were obviously getting ready to move out. Jack felt the noose slip around his neck and he knew that he was going with them. That was good news for the short haul at least. On the trail he was treated like everyone else. He got water at the rest stops and he ate what the troops were eating, if he could just keep up. As if reading Jack's mind, the soldier holding the rope gave it a quick jerk and pulled him to his knees. Then he pulled it again and Jack sprawled face down in the dirt. The soldier put his foot on Jack's neck and held him there. Jack knew better than to offer any resistance, but he couldn't breathe and panic overtook him as he felt the dirt in his mouth and the dust in his lungs. He started to struggle. A shot rang out and the pressure on his neck was lifted. Then the whole area erupted in gunfire. Jack thought he was being executed. The gunfire went on forever in Jack's mind. Actually it lasted about ten seconds. When it abruptly stopped Jack looked up and saw the face of an American.

"Holy shit. Where did you guys come from?"

Other Americans were already melting back into the jungle. Two of them came over to Jack and helped him to his feet. They asked if he could walk. There were dead V.C. all over the place. All of his captors were dead.

"Let's go." It was the tall American he had seen at first who gave the order. "We have to get the hell out of here."

There was a bizarre quality about his rescuers. They wore jungle fatigues; their faces were smeared with camouflage grease. Some wore bush hats. Others had sweatbands tied around their heads. One wore a camouflage bandana tied tightly over his skull. They handled their weapons easily and casually and they moved with catlike grace. There was practically no talk yet each seemed to know what the others were thinking. And they were deadly. More than a dozen Charlies lying in the dirt attested to that. These guys came out of nowhere and killed a squad of VC in less time than it takes to tell about it. The VC probably didn't even get off a shot.

Jack started to move off with the others and suddenly stopped short. Propped against a tree where he had been sitting just before he died was the interrogator. Strangely, Jack felt sorry for him. He had been good at his job, a real pro; a rotten son of a bitch, but a real pro.

"Move it." The voice was commanding. It was almost a threat. It seemed to say get moving or we'll leave you here. Thirty or forty seconds could not have elapsed since the marine reconnaissance team had broken into the clearing to rescue Jack and they were all moving down the trail toward the sea.

"Don't make a sound until I tell you that you can talk." The sun had just broken through the eastern sky and Jack could see the hard face of the team leader. The voice came without emotion or expression, but to Jack it meant that if he didn't do as expected he might end up on the trail with a knife in his ribs. He was more afraid now than he had been marching with the VC with a noose around his neck.

Jack had run into some of these recon people down in the shacks that passed for bars in Da Nang. He tried to avoid them because they were a mean tempered bunch. Even in the bars they stuck together as a team. If something happened that they didn't like they went quiet. Then one of them would deliver a message. It could be anything. The music was too loud; the music was not loud enough. There were too many people in the bar. There weren't enough women for them. Anything could set them off. If things didn't change to their liking instantly the shit hit the fan. Sometimes it was over quickly. Sometimes it took a squad of MPs to sort things out. It depended on who else was in the bar and how tough they were. Jack remembered the poster on the wall of one bar. It had a picture of a caricatured recon marine with the inscription under it "Yea though I walk through the shadow of the valley of death, I shall fear no evil 'cause I'm the meanest son of a bitch in the valley."

Jack felt that silence now. And he had been given the message. This was just another job for the team. It wasn't a mission of mercy with honor and glory for the Corps spurring them on. They had been given a briefing the day before that a corporal down at the hospital had given some pretty fair directions to an area where a navy officer may be held prisoner. The area had been scouted by plane and there were three likely spots where descriptions matched terrain and buildings. Intelligence selected the most likely of the three and the recon team was dropped in by helicopter about two miles away just after sunset the night before. It was a one in three chance to find the officer. If he wasn't there, their orders were to get some prisoners and maybe some light could be shed on his whereabouts. So the recon patrol would have been just as happy to be bringing back three or four VC prisoners.

They moved at a quick pace down the trail. The patrol knew they could handle just about any force they might meet in this area. These were all small bands of VC foraging in the area and keeping the locals in line. They also harassed the American and South Vietnamese in small groups. Sometimes they banded together with other groups for larger scale assaults. Right now they were broken up and scattered all over hell's half acre so that the American military muscle couldn't be brought to bear against them. But that made it easier for the recon patrols to operate in their territory as well. Had the VC been concentrating their forces Jack couldn't have been rescued as easily; in fact, he wouldn't have been left in the isolated village for so long. He would have been brought to a central prisoner area.

Jack did his best to keep up, but the hell he had been through didn't leave him much to work with.

"I have to stop for a minute," he finally told the team leader. The paranoia that came with lack of sleep led Jack to think that they would leave him if he couldn't keep up. He went as long as he could but he had a terrible pain in his side that hurt to the point of frightening him.

Almost without breaking stride, two marines rigged a stretcher that they had with them just for this purpose. They weren't about to carry him unnecessarily, but once they realized that he was hurt they would carry him a million miles to get him back to friendly lines. Marines were like that. They could be a real pain in the ass, but when it came to sticking together there was no force in the world that could match them. They would rather die than leave their wounded. It was the glue that held them together. They knew that they could depend on each other. As long as Jack was with them he had nothing to worry about. It had never occurred to the team leader or any other member of the team that they weren't going to get Jack out, much less that they would leave him under any circumstances. Jack's paranoia about being left was not one of their problems.

Being carried on a stretcher with two guys dog trotting is no bed of roses. Jack thought he might be better off walking. "Put me down, I'll try to make it walking."

"No time. We're almost to the LZ." The team leader was already in the landing zone talking to the chopper pilot on the radio. The rule was to have everything ready when the chopper hit the ground. The helicopter was vulnerable enough in the air. On the ground it was a big fat target that you could disable with a slingshot if you got the rock into the rotor blades at just the right angle. When the team leader saw the stretcher party break into the clearing he called the chopper in.

The crew was helping the recon team aboard before the skids hit the ground. Jack was tossed in through the side door, stretcher and all and his two bearers clamored in beside him. They were still struggling to get everyone aboard when the pilot lifted off and headed for Da Nang.

CHAPTER 10

By the time the word arrived that Jeff was back in American hands and safe, things had eased up bit around the Dunlay house. Anita was regaining some of her self-control. Susie had been doing fine in spite of the recent chaos. Phil had been drinking more than usual, but everyone tried to ignore it. Les was spending more and more time at the Berkeley campus of the University of California. He had become caretaker of Jeff's truck after turning sixteen and getting his driver's license. Had things been normal Les would never have gotten the freedom he enjoyed lately. He was taking full advantage of his newfound mobility. He also found that he fit in well with the campus radicals at Berkeley. No one asked his age when he started hanging around. Everyone assumed that he was a student at the University. The fact that he frequently disappeared to some unknown place just added to his mystique. He had even met a few 'older' women around the campus. One of them was eager to teach him the ways of the world. Les told his parents he was staying overnight with friends, which was true in a way, and he was often away in Berkeley. His parents normally knew to ask the right questions to get the right answers. Les wouldn't lie, but he felt no moral need to answer questions that weren't asked. The way things had been going the past month he probably could have admitted to shacking up in a waterfront whorehouse with an insane transvestite and it wouldn't have registered.

"Hey, Les, you puke; got any grass, man?"

Les didn't like the Senator. That was the name the group had given to the skinny, rather homely young man sitting on the floor pecking away on a portable typewriter. "I don't use the stuff, Senator."

"Keeps you mellow, man. Makes life worthwhile. A pound of grass, a piece of ass, and thou beside me in the student union. That's Omar fucking Cayuga, man. Sure you don't have some grass?"

Les had to laugh. The Senator had a way with words. A pound of grass and a piece of ass. He'd have to remember that and tell Jeff when he saw him. For an instant the shabby room contrasted with everything he knew and it didn't seem right to be thinking of his brother while he was here. The thought passed. "Sorry, Senator. Mary will be here soon. She usually has some in her purse."

The Senator was the quintessential radical. Even to his looks. He wore his hair long and took pride in never being quite clean. He wore those funny little round glasses, and his teeth were stained. He looked like an absolute degenerate bum, and in a way he was. But beneath the exterior facade laid a keen mind. He would probably never do anything worthwhile. His purpose in life was to upset the establishment. Never ever conform. Years later when real senators would wear their hair long, our Senator would shave his head, grow a belly button length beard and have an absolutely filthy word tattooed on his ear. That would be after he got out of prison for bombing a draft board headquarters.

One by one the members of the group wandered into the room. It was in a seedy building in a run down neighborhood. The kind of neighborhood where the police left things alone unless forced to take action. They really hoped the inhabitants would kill each other off during the night. When one or two were found expired on the street or in an alley for whatever reason, the police showed up but their investigations weren't particularly probing.

The group was equally divided between males and females not counting Les. He liked to think of himself as the thirteenth member. Actually he had been the tenth person to join the group, but thirteen sounded better to him. There was a lot of talk and the members made big plans to bring down the government, stop the war, harass the police, take over the University, and bring on the "revolution". Except for one of the males pissing on a police car and getting arrested, they never did anything. They assembled, loaded up on marijuana, beer, wine, or whatever was available and passed out. This night was no different and Les found himself driving home earlier than usual.

Susie met Les in the driveway when he pulled in. She jumped in the truck and directed him to the hospital. Their mother had been taking various medications to calm her nerves. The pills were working and in a spirit of reconciliation she had decided to have a couple of drinks with her husband. The sedatives, nerve pills, and alcohol were a bad combination. Anita had collapsed on the living room floor and Phil couldn't revive her. His judgment was a bit fuzzy, but he got her to the emergency room at the hospital in a breakneck drive across town.

Phil was in the waiting room when Susie and Les arrived. They embraced and cried and all three of them realized that they needed each other as a family. One of the doctors came out and told them that they should go home and rest. Anita was responding to treatment and would be fine, but for now there was nothing more the family could do.

★ ★ ★

Tony Karpaski's Casualty Assistance Calls responsibility covered a broad geographical range. Many were in a military housing complex. They had accounted for over half of the twenty-six CACO calls he had made in the past two years. The others were made in private homes and apartments from where young men and women had gone off to defend the nation.

Each of the services has its own set of standards for notifying next of kin. The navy's rules require that an officer make its calls. If at all possible, the officer should be senior to the person being reported on. Another rule precluded making calls between 10:00 pm and 6:00 am. The CACO officer could be contacted at any time and for some reason most cases got to him after midnight. He had to make the call as soon as possible, so it usually meant a sleepless night. It was recommended that a chaplain accompany the CACO officer, but reserve centers didn't have chaplains so Tony made most of his calls alone.

There was no easy way to make the notification. Tony had seen all kinds. Sometimes relatives were adding up the insurance money and dividing a decedent's property right there on the spot. One father was sure his son was a victim of foul play. It took a personal phone call from the admiral and an investigation by the man's senator to close the file on that one. More than a few of the people that Tony had called on held him personally responsible for the death he was reporting. He never knew what to expect as he made the lonely drive to a next of kin's house. The official notification went something like: "Mrs. Smith, it is my duty on behalf of the Secretary of the Navy to report to you that your son, Robert, was killed in action two days ago in Viet Nam. May I offer the condolences of a grateful nation to you in this moment of your loss?"

There were some CACOs that could get through all that without gagging. Tony was not one of them. He figured that the last thing the mother of a young man taken in the prime of life needed was some second hand message from a Washington political appointee and a lot of bullshit about how grateful the whole nation was for the way her son went out to defend his country but wasn't coming back. It might have worked during World War II, but Viet Nam was something different. Some cases were really bizarre. He reported, as ordered, an accidental death by gunshot on one young sailor when he knew the truth was that the man had killed himself playing Russian roulette in the guard shack where he was standing duty.

What could the country be grateful for anyway. Some poor slob went half way around the world to another country to get his ass shot off by a guy who lived there. What did people expect. What would we do if 500,000 Chinese soldiers showed up in San Diego?

Tony played every call by ear. He made up his little talk on the spot depending on the circumstances. If parents were involved, he tried to get them together before breaking the news. If it was a wife, he warned her that he had news about her husband and gave her time to get the kids where she wanted them. His navy car and his uniform usually alerted people that there was something wrong. They prepared themselves for a shock. Usually, but not always. Once he pulled in to a small town gas station and asked for the owner by name. A smiling man in his forties greeted him and invited him into the office. He was expecting the bite to be put on him for some kind of navy donation. Maybe some help with a recruiting display or something like that. He was friendly and outgoing, a generous man that had no idea that the stranger before him was going to rip a piece out of his heart. This naval officer for whom he had respect and admiration, even though he had never seen him before, was going to take his dearest possession away from him forever. Tony was speechless for a moment. Normally people were apprehensive about his visit. They prepared for something bad, some unpleasant news at best. But this man with his bright, optimistic smile was totally unprepared. Tony shifted from one foot to the other when the man asked what he could do for him. "Anything for our men in blue, Commander." he had said. Tony had to tell him that it wasn't that simple. He had to tell him that he had the worst possible news about his son. He had been killed in an automobile accident in Viet Nam.

The father had been stunned. For a moment he couldn't talk or move. But he was too kind a person to be vindictive or rude even at a time like that. He asked Tony to wait outside while he called his wife. When he came out of the office, he asked Tony to come home with him. Tony followed the man to his house. Friends and family had already gathered. Even the local undertaker, a friend of the family, was there. He was insisting on taking care of all arrangements free of charge. Tony explained the procedures the navy followed in these cases: burial payments, headstones, preparation of the remains, the casket. There was need for an honor guard, arrangements with the family church, and so forth. The undertaker assured Tony that everything would be taken care of. As a casualty officer, Tony usually remained aloof and kept his association with the family on a formal basis. He couldn't afford to take on the pain time and time again. But this one got to him. Less than a week later the young man's remains were delivered home.

On a balmy autumn day the breeze rustled the canopy over the seating area where the family joined in their sorrow. The minister's words were from Psalms 5:9:

"...remember this fine young man. Direct O Lord, my God, his way in thy sight."

Next came the military ritual. The orders to the firing squad: "Ready, aim, fire. Aim, fire. Aim, fire. Order arms."

Family members were still wincing from the unexpected volleys from the honor guard rifles when the doleful melody of Taps echoed across the valley. The flag that had draped the coffin was properly folded by the American Legion members and handed to Commander Karpaski. He carried it to the boy's mother and handed it to her. He was supposed to say "Please accept this flag, the symbol of our country, on behalf of a grateful nation." But the only words that he could force out of his throat were "Dear Lord, I'm so sorry." Tears welled in his eyes. The mother's gentle squeeze on his arm and the father's pat on his back told him that the words made no difference. This time Tony took on the pain and it was terrible.

Karpaski couldn't remember what had set him off thinking about CACOs past. It happened often, particularly during the long drives to make the calls. But this time wasn't going to be bad. He was going to tell Mrs. Walker that her husband was coming home. He had been rescued by a marine recon team and was currently in the hospital in Da Nang. His condition was good and he would be on his way home soon.

Sally flopped in a chair, looked Tony right in the eye and said: "Oh, shit, Commander. That's good news!"

Sally worked her pregnant body out of the chair and went to the phone. "Stand by, Commander. I'll buy you a drink in a minute, but first I have to tell a friend about the good news."

Susie had called Sally a few days before and told her that Jeff had been found. Now it was Sally's turn. The phone rang just as she reached for it. Sally was bubbling as she answered it, but her mood changed almost immediately. "Fuck you, you miserable turd." Tony's jaw dropped and he stood openmouthed staring at Sally.

The person on the phone had called to tell Sally that he and his friends hadn't forgotten about her and her warmonger husband. He was used to having the upper hand in these conversations, but Sally's explosive response threw him off. It was one thing to harass a distraught, pregnant woman, but this was unexpected, the voice on the phone waivered. He made another attempt to harangue Sally, but she was clearly in control. She worked the caller like a fish on a hook. Her mind was clicking like a well-oiled clock. Keep this bastard on the line and give Delcarthy's boys time to trace the call. She dropped the bravado and turned vulnerable. She played it just right. The call got traced. She would get a crack at her tormenter in court. What a day. By the time she got through to Susie she was in ecstasy.

Poor Tony was dumbstruck. Every other time he had called on Sally she was recovering from some blow he had given her. She was either flat on her back in a hospital or trying to cope with her toddler son and terrible news at the same time. This time she was laughing and winking and making punching gestures worthy of a middleweight. This made up for all the lousy CACO calls he had ever had to make.

CHAPTER 11

Jeff was recovering, but he suffered a major setback. His foot had become too badly infected to save. The doctor amputated his leg halfway between the ankle and the knee. They explained it to him after the operation. Another week and he would lose the whole leg, or worse. There weren't any consent forms or doctor-patient heart to heart talks in front line hospitals. The whole place was one big emergency ward. Some people made it, others died. Jeff felt lousy about losing his lower leg, but in the context of where he was it didn't seem that bad. That kind of thinking might change later, but considering where he was and what he had been through, Jeff wasn't going to dwell on his loss. All around him was suffering and anguish. Burns, gunshot wounds, men blinded, parts missing.

Jeff surveyed the scene. "This sure isn't like the movies show it," he thought to himself. In the movies the heroes have a private room, a pretty nurse, and sparkling white sheets. They take their wounds stoically. They never cry or scream. They rarely bleed and they never vomit or shit their pants. "I wonder how all this would go over at a Saturday matinee? The movies would never show that guy across from me with the holes in his chest and the big purple marks left by a really lousy stitching job when they sewed him back up. Look at those scars and blood soaked bandages." One thing the movies could never convey to the audience is the smell. That would sure as hell empty the theatre. Most people never even see an emergency room much less an evacuation hospital in a war zone. Even if they think they know what it is like, they really haven't a clue to the real thing.

Under the circumstances, Jeff was being as stoic as one could expect. He wasn't in much pain and the staff treated him pretty well. No one pulled rank. They were all reduced to a common denominator by the blue pajamas on the patients and the green, surgical pajamas on the medical staff, or vice versa depending on the laundry schedule. When it got hectic, those who were able chipped in and helped with the duties. Walking patients helped clean up messes and console the new arrivals. The blue and green pajamas blended under the blood spattered on them. There were times when there seemed to be blood everywhere except where it belonged.

The thing that bothered Jeff the most was that he would have been on his way home except for the damned foot. When things turned bad it was decided to keep him in Da Nang rather than risk a medevac to the big hospital in Japan. Now, sheer numbers from the VC Tet offensive were clogging the evacuation routes and Jeff was on hold.

"Nurse, sir."

"It's either nurse, ma'am, or lieutenant. Don't push your luck, corporal."

In spite of all his easy-going charm, Jeff wasn't really a lady's man. He was a bit bashful. He hid it by clowning around and most women he met considered him cute and harmless. Nurse Jamison was a navy nurse lieutenant in her mid twenties, crusty on the surface but a marshmallow underneath. Good looking, and according to most marines, built like a bamboo shithouse. He talked to her every time he got a chance and she was beginning to notice that he got the chance quite often lately.

"Nurse, sir. I wanted to ask you about the guy at the end of the ward. The one trussed up like a chicken. He never talks to anyone and not many people talk to him. Is he hurt bad?"

"He's hurt worse than anyone here. One of his officers shot him."

"An accident?"

"Not hardly. I don't have the whole story. He's facing a court martial for desertion under fire. That's why he was shot." Nurse Jamison's gaze down the ward was compassionate.

"That's the dumbest thing I ever heard of. Where the hell is anyone going to desert to in this part of the world?"

"Corporal, you have a way of going right to the heart of things. His name is Pete. Maybe you could use some of that Irish charm of yours to try to reach him. He could use a friend."

Nurse Helen Jamison considered herself a pretty good judge of character. She thought Jeff might be the one to relate to the sad young fellow at the end of the ward. She had tried to get some of the others to talk to Pete, but they were all too angry and bitter about their own wounds to reach out to a deserter. She thought Jeff might be different. Jeff gave her a smile and his eyes drifted to her well-shaped breasts. Before she could admonish him he said, "If you bring me a chair I'll roll down and talk to him, Nurse, sir."

* * *

Lieutenant Jack Walker had been brought in to the hospital for a physical. In spite of his experience, he was in good shape. The pain in his side that downed him on the trail when the marines were bringing him out was persisting. He thought that maybe he had suffered a broken rib when the interrogator beat him, but the doctors assured him that it was only a bad bruise. There might have been a slight crack, but it wasn't broken.   The Recon Team had disappeared the minute the chopper hit the deck in Da Nang. He got a quick debriefing by the local intelligence people and was hurried on to a plane bound for Saigon. Jack's priority had been to call Sally, but he was told that the military priority was his seat on the plane. He could phone from Saigon. MACV Staff Intelligence wanted to debrief him and find out what they could about the VC taking so many prisoners. Jack's plane arrived at Tan Son Nhut airport shortly after noon on January 31st, the day of the Tet offensive. Some VC hiding in a building overlooking the airport cut loose with a recoilless rocket just as the plane touched down. The rocket caught the landing gear and exploded under the left wing. Shrapnel peppered the plane and the left wheel was blown off. The pilot tried to compensate as the left wing dipped to the ground but before he could do anything the plane slewed to the left and the right landing gear took the full brunt of the plane's weight in a sideways skid. It collapsed. The C-47 flopped on its belly and skidded to a grinding halt. The old workhorse had flown its last mission, but everyone aboard was home safely one last time. The passengers and crew scrambled out and ran to get off the exposed runway. Jack was beginning to wonder if he was going to make it out of Viet Nam alive.

The spooks (as intelligence people are affectionately known) at MACV did a cursory debriefing. The offensive told them what they needed to know about the VC taking prisoners. Jack was given another set of orders sending him back to Da Nang, but things at the airport were a bit confused and the only traffic moving was direct support and offensive aircraft. The only passengers were front line troops going to whatever area appeared to be a front line.

Jack found a billet at one of the hotels assigned to visiting officers. It wasn't an encouraging sight when his driver dropped him off. The hotel was surrounded with a ten-foot high wire fence topped with concertina razor wire. South Vietnamese troops were assigned to guard the hotel and there was one posted every ten feet. None of them looked too interested in the job. Jack's army driver explained that they all had political pull and the guard duty was preferable to jungle duty. "They're useless." was the driver's opinion. "Their whole damned army is useless. You ever have to work with those yahoos, Lieutenant?"

Jack didn't answer the question. His mind flashed back to a conversation with Fixcue when the latter had returned from Bangkok on R & R. Fixcue had gotten a taxi to take him to his hotel and he engaged in a conversation with the driver. Turns out the driver was from My Tho, a city south of Saigon. He had fled to Thailand when the American buildup started. The United States was demanding that the South Vietnamese government take a greater part in the war. The draft of young men was stepped up and the driver was afraid that he was going to be conscripted into the army. The irony of the draft dodging Vietnamese driving visiting American fighting men around Bangkok wasn't lost on Fixcue and he made a marvelous story out of it. Jack supposed that the young soldiers around the hotel weren't as resourceful as the taxi driver. People were the same everywhere. Some did what was asked of them and others skirted society's rules. Only history could answer who was closer to being right.

Jack thanked the driver for the lift and made his way into the hotel. The first thing that greeted him was a small bar in the corner of the large entry room. The bar was tended by a smiling old man with several large yellow teeth and a number of gaps that teeth once occupied. He smiled at Jack and pointed to his wares. He evidently didn't speak English, but he knew what people wanted when they visited his little corner. Jack pointed to a bottle of decent scotch and held up his hand with the thumb and forefinger about three inches apart; the he indicated the water pitcher and this time the fingers were almost touching. The smiling man knew exactly what this officer was looking for. He poured Jack a real jolt and indicated that it was on the house when Jack started to get his wallet out. A voice behind him said, "The first one is always free. Most people sent to this prison need a stiff drink more than anything." Before Jack could turn around a friendly arm clasped his shoulder and he saw a hand in front of him being offered to shake. "Not only that, I'll buy the second round. I don't know why the hell you're here, but you're the only drinking buddy I've got. Everyone else is off fighting a damned war some place."

"I'm waiting for a flight out." Jack told his new buddy. The guy was obviously a few drinks ahead of everyone in Saigon, but he had the friendly look that people take to immediately. "Let me take a raincheck on that second round for a bit. I have to find my room and take a shower, if that happens to be an option around here."

"Pick any room you want. All the showers are down the hall unless you pick the General's Suite. Even I haven't worked up enough Dutch courage to do that. Name's Buck. Air Force. I was on my way for a week of R & R with the family when this latest dust-up started. Can't go forward, won't go backward. I'm stuck. Go get your damned shower and lets check this town out. I hear they got women here that do things that make your toes curl in delight."

The only woman Jack was interested in was Sally. Especially after talking to her on the phone earlier from the headquarters building. Their conversation was cut short by higher priority traffic, but he was able to tell her that he was in good health and on the way home soon. He knew that women were only a hand wave away in Saigon, but even the fabled exotic beauty of Vietnamese women in their traditional Au Dai dresses slit to the top of their lovely thighs wasn't going to entice him. If all went well, he would be back in the States in a week or so. He was officially a former prisoner of war and that was a ticket home. After all he had been through, one more week without a woman was something he could handle easily. "I'll join you for booze and food, Buck, but the women are all yours."

"Hell, buddy, I just want to look. No harm in that. Go get your damned shower. Time's a wastin'."

"Are you sure there are places open right now? I just had a plane shot out from under me at the field."

"One thing they don't do in Saigon is close down because of war. These people have been dealing with this stuff for so long it comes with the menu."

Jack spent a leisurely hour sipping his drink, enjoying the hot shower, and just having a few minutes to reflect on what his life had become in the past month. He needed a good rip-roaring night on the town. His wardrobe consisted of a pair of wash khakis and a blue polo shirt. That was all he needed for what he had in mind. It sure as hell wouldn't be a night at the Embassy.

Buck was waiting when he got back to the lobby. They had a quick drink in the little corner bar and headed out into the warm, late afternoon. It was common knowledge that Americans were often targeted by sappers on motor bikes. The driver would pull up to the curb and his passenger on the back would fire a pistol point blank at the victim. Then the motor bike roared away and melted into the heavy traffic of the Saigon streets leaving a dead American in a pool of blood. The same thing could happen to someone riding in a cab, but at least you were a fast moving target most of the time. The two revelers decided to ride. Buck knew all the local spots having spent the last 48 hours on almost continual patrol from one watering hole to another.

They eventually ended up at a French restaurant that was owned and operated by the same family that ran the place when the area was known as French Indo China. They had so far outlasted Japanese, French, and several layers of Vietnamese officialdom -- not to mention the American influence. Through it all they were known for marvelous cuisine. Jack and Buck indulged themselves in hors d'oeuvres, soups, salads, and entrees of succulent meat and vegetables adorned with delicate sauces. Wine flowed through all the courses and brandy and cigars topped the meal. Jack told Buck about his capture and time he spent as a prisoner. The two had more in common that they realized at first. Buck had spent two days evading V.C. patrols when his Phantom jet was shot out of the sky on a low-level support mission. That was two years ago on his first tour of duty in country. He evaded capture and made it home, but the memory of that time never left him. He admitted that he drank a good deal more on his off hours on this tour than on his first tour before he was shot down.

The two wandered out into the balmy evening air and over to another restaurant that had an outdoor patio secluded from the street. A good place to drink and talk. As the conversation bounced from topic to topic, Buck became more serious. He was staring at a particularly beautiful woman seated at a nearby table with a doughy-faced civilian. The man was consulting some notes and ignoring his lovely companion.

"It upsets my C'hi to see something like that."

"It upsets your what?"

"My C'hi."

"What the hell is your C'hi?"

"Don't you navy types know anything about the cultures of the lands you try to conquer?"

"I'm not trying to conquer anything. I'm just doing what my superiors tell me to do. And no one has mentioned your C'hi to me since I got here."

"Have you heard of Yin and Yang. Surely your superiors told you about Yin and Yang."

"I've heard of it. Some kind of Chinese thing."

"All things in the universe are backed by shade, the soft, female, retreating Yin. And they are faced by light, the forceful, driving, male Yang. And they all come into harmony through C'hi." Buck sat back, very satisfied with himself for remembering his little soliloquy about Yin and Yang.

"That may not be anything my superiors told me but it's the longest line of bullshit I've heard since I got here. I thought you were an airplane pilot, not a fucking philosopher."

"The universe is in harmony and we are part of that harmony. When you act in a way that violates the harmony, you upset the balance. Like that dumb shit over there ignoring that beautiful piece of ass. He's upsetting the harmony of the universe."

"Not to mention your C'hi."

"Shit. I think I'll go home and go to bed. I may be able to catch a ride to Hawaii tomorrow. A little R & R with my missus will restore my harmony. Maybe get the whole universe back on track."

Jack was not sure he was going to be able to walk if he got up. This had been a bigger night of drinking than he had planned on and it had been a long time between drinks. "I hope to hell they put you on a plane tomorrow. I can't take another night like this."

The two of them staggered out into the street, oblivious to any potential harm. They smiled at the street-walkers and gave them a friendly pat on the rear end, but they kept walking. Beggars found a soft touch as the two emptied their pockets of what few coins and bills they had left. They finally made it back to the hotel. As Jack pulled himself up the stairs by the handrail, he saw Buck over his shoulder ordering one last drink from the smiling little bartender who never seemed to be away from his station. That was the last time Jack saw Buck. He never even learned his last name. Interesting guy. "Hope the war doesn't kill him."

CHAPTER 12

"Here's your coffee, sir. Just the way you like it; one sugar and a splash of cream. Sir, I wish you'd try drinking it black. The men are starting to talk."

"Just put the cup down and go check on the mail. And one more crack about my coffee drinking habits and you'll need a surgeon to remove the cup. What the hell do you people do out there all morning? It takes you half the day to sort out a few letters and get them delivered."

Parker backed out the door doing a little vaudeville shuffle and a half salute closing the door gently behind him as Commander Karpaski bellowed his displeasure. Considering tradition and the navy's rules about officers and enlisted personnel fraternizing socially, Yeoman First Class Parker and Commander Karpaski were pretty good friends. Parker was a crackerjack yeoman with eighteen years of experience running the ship's office, the hub of administrative activity. Navy tradition dictated that it was a "ship's office" even when the office was at a shore base. All the records were kept there and whoever ran the ship's office knew everything about the command. Parker would have been a Chief Petty Officer if service, experience and knowledge were all that counted. But he had a serious proclivity for wine, women, and associated habits that slowed his climb up the advancement ladder. In fact, on one occasion he fell all the way to the bottom of the ladder and had to start over again. Karpaski would trust Parker with his life, but he wouldn't let him near his wife or daughter without a police escort

"What's the old man yelling about?" Parker's assistant knew that the boss liked to explain what was happening in the Captain's office, or in some cases, keep people aware that he was the only one who knew what was really going on but couldn't disclose the information.

"He's got that bug up his ass about his orders. Makes me check the mail ten times a day."

"How come he volunteered for Nam? He's got the world by the balls here. You do all the work for him. All he has to do is come and sign his name a few times and he can goof off for the rest of the day."

Parker was a sharpie, but he was a sucker for flattery. His assistant knew that if he could get him talking he wouldn't have to do any work until after lunch.

"How the hell do I know why he volunteered. He's an officer. They do strange things sometimes. He's smart. Went to college and everything. Just no horse sense, I guess."

"How do you rate him as far as Skipper's go?"

Parker was working his way through the paper blizzard that swirled around his desk. "He's one of the best. If he was back in D.C. running things we wouldn't have all this fucking paper to deal with every day. Don't tell him I said this, but he would have made a hell of a good yeoman."

The office door flew open. "Goddammit, Parker. Where's the mail?"

"I'm working on it, sir. Anything in particular you were interested in?"

"You know damned well I'm looking for my orders. If you were any kind of a yeoman I wouldn't have to be out here doing your work for you."

Tony Karpaski went back into his office and slumped in his chair. He was thinking about his decision to volunteer. It had all come to a head a while back when he went up to the local beanery for dinner. It was a drill night. The work day ended at 4:30 and the naval reservists started showing up for training about 6:30 p.m. That was 1830 navy time but Karpaski liked to rag Parker about all his spit and polish navy image stuff so he used civilian time whenever he remembered to do it. There were usually details needing attention on drill night so there wasn't enough time to go all the way home for dinner; he would usually end up at Ma Gorsky's Diner.

Karpaski had to steel himself every time he went through the door to the diner. Mrs. Gorsky was a nice lady and a great cook. She was always friendly and showed Tony the latest letter from her son. The boy had worked at the diner, washing dishes and waiting on the counter. He had gotten to know Tony and the rest of the crew from the reserve center so it was a natural thing for him to sign up in the naval reserve. Rather than take a chance on getting drafted into the army and being sent to Viet Nam, he would be on navy duty for two years and then back to the reserve center for the remainder of his six-year obligation. Except the navy had a way of changing the best laid plans. Young Gorsky ended up in the Seabees and he was now in Viet Nam. All the recruiting talk and the information that Tony had given him about being better off in the navy sounded like a damned lie now.

But Mrs. Gorsky was proud of her son and prouder yet of the fact that he wrote to her at least twice a week and always assured her that he was safe and nowhere near the fighting. Tony knew that there wasn't any place in Viet Nam that was "nowhere near the fighting". But he read the letters and joined Mrs. Gorsky in her discussion about what a fine boy her son was. Tony was sure that one day he was going to walk into that diner and find out that Mrs. Gorsky's fine young son was dead. Then one night it hit him like a punch in the stomach. If anyone was going to notify Mrs. Gorsky that her son was dead, it would have to be Casualty Calls Officer Karpaski. Then he would go back to his safe office and recruit another young man as a replacement. The vision haunted Tony for weeks. One thought led to another and eventually he rationalized that if he was a career officer, then it was logical that he should go to war before he sent anyone else. So why was it taking so long for those bungling bureaucrats in D.C. to cut a set of orders for him? His detailing officer had given him some raz-a-ma-taz about finding a suitable replacement for him and the time it takes to fill the pipeline and all that jargon those people use. Tony figured it should take about 48 hours. There would be a hundred officers happy to grab his job. All that detail officer would have to do is toss a spitball in any direction in the Pentagon and take the first lieutenant commander it hit. It would probably ricochet off of half a dozen suitable replacements.

"Parker! What the hell are you doing out there?"

"Nothing, sir. Just trying to decipher the codes in this set of orders. They sure make it complicated."

"Orders? What orders? Whose orders? God damn it, Parker, do you have my orders out there? Karpaski exploded out of his chair and almost tore the hinges off of the office door. He ripped the papers out of Parker's hands and read his orders. Essentially they read:

From: Bureau of Naval Personnel

To : Lieutenant Commander Anthony L. Karpaski, USN

Subj: Permanent Change of Station

When relieved, on or about 1 May 1968 proceed and report

to the CO NAVPHIBBASE Coronado, CA for training, etc. etc., and then

to Commander First Riverine Detatchment, Da Nang, Viet Nam for duty as Executive Officer, COM RIV etc. etc. 30 days leave etc.

Tony got the gist of the orders, but there was the usual coded jargon that needed checking in the book. "Put this in plain English for me, Parker. ASAP. And keep this under your hat. And that goes for that assistant gorilla of yours. If my wife hears about this before I get a chance to tell her, your ass won't be worth a six inch length of anchor chain. Do you read me, Parker?"

"Aye, aye, sir." Parker was going to ride the old man a bit about his orders, but something in Karpaski's eyes told him that this was no time for jokes; and his last order was no joke either.

Tony went back into his office and sat in his chair rather heavily. Talking about Viet Nam and looking for orders and raising hell with Parker every day was one thing. But reading the words to proceed to war was something else. A shiver passed through Tony and a fear came over him. It was the realization that he was going to go to war and that he could be killed. Now he had to tell his wife about the reality. When he first told her about how he felt she said to do whatever he thought best. But Tony could tell that she was just trying to be a good navy wife and live up to the bargain they struck when they got married. For better or worse and all that business. Now it was happening.

"Parker, I'll be at home if anyone is looking for me, remember what I told you!"

"Yes, sir. My lips are sealed. And that goes for the assistant gorilla too. Here's the English translation. Is it what you wanted?"

"Someone once said 'Be careful what you ask for, you might get it.' I got what I asked for, Parker."

Lieutenant Commander Karpaski sauntered out the front door of the Naval Reserve Center with mixed emotions of elation, fear, freedom, and depression swirling within him. He could barely get his car started. "I need a good stiff drink," he thought. But then he realized that all he needed to do now was get bombed and show up at home staggering and slurring to tell his wife he was off to war and for her not to worry, they don't shoot drunks. He decided against the drink and ten minutes later he was pulling into the familiar drive.

Ellie was working in the garden. The kids were still in school. Tony called out to Ellie but she kept her head down and went on digging in the soft dirt. He called again. No answer. When he got closer he could see that Ellie was crying. "Ellie, what's wrong?" Tony knew what was wrong and for a minute he toyed with the idea of getting back in his car and driving to the Reserve Center and killing Parker.

"You're leaving, aren't you?" Ellie had a hard time getting the words out. She kept stabbing the ground with her little trowel.

"How did you find out? Did that idiot Parker call you?"

"No one called, Tony. I just knew."

This wasn't the first time Ellie "knew" something had happened or was going to happen. She knew that their first child was going to be born with a club-foot. The doctor discounted it as a tragically correct coincidence, but it wasn't. Ellie knew. She knew the time they had left her parents' house after a vacation visit that she would never see her father alive again. He died of a heart attack a month later. Ellie mentioned it on the drive home. There was no discussion or anything. She mentioned it, Tony told her that she was just feeling guilty about not visiting enough, and that was all there was too it. But she knew.

"The orders just came this morning. It took Parker hours to sort the mail. I could have kicked him. I don't know why the hell I wasted my time checking the mail. I could have stayed home and checked with you. Could have stayed in bed and enjoyed myself."

Ellie got up and put her arms around him and held him tighter than she ever had before. "Don't go, Tony. Don't go."

"I have to. The orders are cut. The pipeline is full. I'm part of the machinery. Someone is coming to relieve me. I'm going to relieve someone else. We all have to move one space. It's in the rules."

Ellie gave him a long, sad look and then took his hand and started walking toward the house. She kicked a clod of dirt and then turned to him. "I didn't know that you were going. What I knew was that you weren't coming back."

Tony felt a little sick. He had just had a premonition of his own back at the office. Now his wife, the mystic, was telling him that he was right. He was going to get killed. He took his wife in his arms and held her close to him. "Of course I'm not coming back here. When I finish my tour in Viet Nam I'll be ordered to a new duty station."

Ellie gave him a hard look. "Don't joke with me about this, Tony. I'm serious. If you go, you won't come back."

"This isn't a joke to me, Ellie. I had the same feeling when I read the orders. That's what your psychic mind picked up on. You felt what I felt. But I don't have a record of having premonitions that pan out. So I was probably wrong, and in this case, so are you."

Ellie started walking toward the house. She took a few steps and turned back to Tony. "You bastard. I'll never forgive you if you get killed. I'm going to show you how serious I am about this. I haven't had a drink in the afternoon since before the kids were born. I'm going to have one now and I'll warn you in advance, by the time the sun goes down I'll be drunk as a hoot owl. You take care of the kids, you fix dinner, and you get ready to put me to bed when I pass out. You bastard, you big, God damn navy hero, you owe this to me."

Tony followed her into the house a safe distance. He really felt like he needed a drink himself, but fair was fair. Someone had to look after the kids and he knew his wife well enough to realize that he had better take the responsibility. He owed it to her. He phoned Parker and told him to cover for him if anyone called.

CHAPTER 13

Jeff sat next to the bed of the man accused of desertion under fire. It had been an hour since Nurse Jamison had gotten the wheelchair for him and he wheeled himself down the ward to the bed in the corner. The young man lying on the bed had a cast on his upper body and right arm. The arm cast was attached to a pulley intended to keep him from rolling around and hurting himself. "The poor guy" thought Jeff, "he's got troubles."

Jeff introduced himself but he got no response from Pete. The fellow just lay there and stared at the ceiling. Jeff didn't say anything for a long time. He sat calmly and offered a friendly smile whenever Pete happened to glance his way. Nurse Jamison had told him that Pete probably wouldn't talk. He hadn't said a word since he came out of surgery. Well over an hour had elapsed when Jeff decided to call it a day. Before wheeling himself off, Jeff leaned over to Pete and said "Listen, man, you've got some problems you need to talk about. I'll be back later."

Nurse Jamison was near Jeff's bed when he got back. "Any luck?"

"He didn't say a word. I'm gong to go back later and see if I can get him into a game of gin rummy or something." Jeff glanced down the ward and saw a navy officer in summer whites standing at Pete's bed. "Hey, Nurse Sir, Pete's got a visitor."

"Must be his attorney. I had a note they were sending someone over today. I better go check." She came back a few minutes later and told Jeff that he better hurry up if he wanted to play gin rummy. "That officer said that Headquarters had ordered a pre-trial screening and that the prosecutor would be taking depositions in a day or two."

The lieutenant in summer whites was Pete's defense council. He had arrived in Viet Nam two weeks ago. He completed his officer orientation and Judge Advocate General (JAG) training shortly after graduating from law school and was sent to JAG Headquarters in Da Nang. It was obvious that someone high up was madder than hell at Pete and wasn't going to give him any kind of a break. They were pushing the trial as fast as possible and they picked the low man on the totem pole to defend him.

"That poor guy would have been better off if his officer had been a better shot and put one in his head. I've had a little experience in front of a judge, but nothing like this guy is facing."

Nurse Jamison's jaw dropped. "What do you mean, you've had experience in front of a judge? What kind of trouble could a sweet kid like you get into?" She hadn't meant to get personal and it was obvious to Jeff that she started blushing the minute the "sweet kid" comment slipped out.

"Why Nurse Sir, I think you're sweet too." Jeff pressed his advantage when he saw how flustered Nurse Jamison was getting. "I had no idea you felt that way about me. Want to pop into the X-Ray room and see what develops?"

"I'd order a cold shower for you if it wasn't for that bad leg. Shape up, corporal. You're talking to an officer." Nurse Jamison walked down the ward and checked a few charts, straightened out a few blankets, and then disappeared behind the screen that separated the duty nurse's desk from the ward. She peeked out between the screen panels and saw Jeff lying on his bed looking very contented with himself.

Jeff ate dinner at his bed. He was going to go down and see Pete after the evening meal, but he fell asleep and it was time for lights out when the corpsman woke him to take his medication. He decided to wait until morning to try again.

The next morning, Jeff spent a few minutes after breakfast telling Nurse Jamison about his youthful misdeeds and how Judge Banes gave him the choice of the Marine Corps or lord knows what. It was the first time that he had realized that he had no idea what punishment Judge Banes had in mind for him.

All hell broke loose just as he was finishing his story. Choppers were landing with wounded and Nurse Jamison, along with everyone else on the staff flew into action to take care of the new wounded. Everything was happening outside the ward and in surgery. Jeff and the other recovering wounded were on their own during these periods unless there was a critical case in the ward. At the moment things were fairly stable and the staff felt they could leave the ward and do more good with the new arrivals.

Jeff worked his way out of bed and into his wheel chair. Pete's attorney had come in and had spent a few minutes talking to him. He left by the back door and Jeff wheeled himself down the ward. "How ya doin', Pete?" Jeff was hoping that he could get a conversation going since Pete had been talking to the officer.

"I'd be better off dead. Semper Fi doesn't extend to cowards." Semper Fi is the shortened version of the Marine Corps motto Semper Fidelis which is Latin for Always Faithful. Marines use it to explain the vagueness of life the way Christians use the term "It's God's will."

"You're in a tough spot, but whatever happens it's better than being dead. There were a few times in the past month when I might have agreed with you, but if I had given up I wouldn't be sitting here waiting to go home. You've got to stick it out."

The young man lying on the bed started to cry. "That's what it's all about. You didn't give up, even when you were wounded. You're a hero. You didn't run away." The words came rushing out in a torrent with the tears.

Jeff wanted to cry himself. He could see his little brother in the other man's eyes. The poor guy obviously wasn't a fighter. That had never bothered Jeff. He could fight, but he didn't like it. And he never picked a fight with someone who couldn't defend himself. The first schoolyard fight he ever got into wasn't to defend himself, it was because he was standing up for another boy who was being picked on. He wasn't a bully and he could understand the man who just couldn't bring himself to swing a fist. "I'm no hero, and you're probably not a coward. What happened to you?"

"Don't try to make it look right. I am a coward. I always have been. I ran away from every fight anyone ever tried to start with me."

"Then what the hell are you doing in the Corps? Didn't you read the literature they handed out?"

The young man wiped his face with a wash rag and looked Jeff in the eye. "It was my father's idea. He said they would make a man out of me. He shamed me into enlisting. He said he didn't want anything to do with me if I was going to be a chicken all my life. I knew it was a mistake, but I had to try. During Boot Camp I even thought I might be changing a bit. On our first liberty I got drunk and got in a fight with some sailor. It wasn't much of a brawl. The Shore Patrol broke us up before anyone got hurt and sent us back to camp. After that I thought that maybe I had broken the barrier."

Jeff smiled. "Sounds like a start. But what happened to get you shot?"

"I couldn't take it. I broke. We were under fire and I ran. I was so scared I didn't know what I was doing."

"Where were you, out on patrol?"

"No, I was with Headquarters Company. I'm a clerk. We were out on an inspection trip. Wasn't supposed to be any action. I haven't fired a rifle since training. We carried M-16s out on inspections, but mine wasn't even loaded. I had to carry so God damn many books and inspection forms around that I didn't have the strength to carry ammunition too. Shit, I've been in Country for seven months and I hadn't gotten near a bullet, ours or theirs, until the Captain shot me."

"But why did he shoot you? Something must have been going on."

"We went out to a forward base, it was a routine inspection trip. We usually went in, did the paperwork, wrote up a bunch of bullshit and left. Only this time Charlie hit the base while we were counting the paper clips. I could see that the Captain was as scared as I was. He had never been in a firefight either. He had managed to wangle staff billets every tour. Someone finally caught up with him and sent him over here. Anyway, when the gooks hit us we were out near the edge of the base looking at the officer's putting green."

"You're shitting me. What do you mean, putting green?"

"That's just what I mean. The base C.O. was a golf nut and the Captain was just as bad. We were out there looking at the fucking putting green and the V.C. hit. There was so much shit going on I don't remember what I did. I kind of remember running, but I'm not sure. Things are kind of a blur until I woke up here. When I woke up I was chained to the bed and some officer told me that I was under arrest for desertion under fire."

"This doesn't make sense. You can't desert from a forward base. There's no place to go."

"I told you. I don't remember. The Captain wrote up the report. He said that when the shooting started, he ..." Before Pete could finish the sentence his lawyer came in and told him to stop talking. He ordered Jeff to leave the area and then went into a serious huddle with Pete.

The conversation went on for almost half and hour and then the officer left. Jeff immediately wheeled himself back down to see Pete. "What's going on now, man?"

"They're shipping me to Tokyo. I'll be on the next medevac plane out. I'm not supposed to say anything, but he just told me that the charges may be dropped. There's a rumor around that I wasn't the one who broke and ran. It was the Captain. He went nuts, shot me and tried to surrender to the V.C. A whole squad got wiped out when they went out to rescue him after he got himself pinned down. The officers were trying to protect him after the firefight stopped. They told everyone to keep quiet about what happened and planned to put the blame on me. They thought I was dead when the dust off chopper hauled me off so they made up the story that I was the one who broke and ran and got the squad killed."

"Didn't anyone see what was going on?"

"I guess not. The officer that ordered the squad out and the Captain were the only survivors in that sector, except for me, and I was out of it while all this was going on."

"So now they're going to ship you out and cover up the whole mess."

"Not only that, I'm probably going to get a Bronze Star and a Purple Heart if I keep my mouth shut and go along with the cover up."

Jeff gave him a long look. "What else would you do?"

"I told you, Jeff. I've always been a coward. I always ran away from a fight. If I take a medal and run this time my life won't be worth shit."

"You can't fight the officers. If they want to bury you, they'll do it. They're protecting one of their own, and if they have to give you a phony citation and a medal to keep the word about a coward officer getting out, they'll do it. You try to fight them and your life will be shit."

"That son of a bitch shot me, he freaked out, and then he tried to pin the whole mess on me. What if I had died and got shipped back to my father with a yellow streak painted on my coffin? It would have killed my old man. I can't take a medal and say forget that it happened. I know what happened. I may not have been a hero, but I don't think I was a coward under fire either."

Jeff was leaning over and protesting to Pete that he was setting himself up for a fragging. He'd never get out of Viet Nam alive if he blew the whistle on the officer. Nurse Jamison came up and heard the last part of Jeff's comment.

She started to wheel Jeff off and said to Pete "You're not supposed to have visitors. Your attorney said that you're in isolation as of now." As she wheeled Jeff back up the ward she leaned over and quietly asked him what the fragging comment was about.

"Fragging? That's when someone who's supposed to be on your side drops a grenade down your shorts." Jeff tried to laugh it off.

"I know what a damned fragging is, I want to know who's going to frag who."

Jeff liked Nurse Jamison and he knew that if it wasn't for her he never would have gone down to talk to Pete, but she was an officer and he couldn't trust her. This was a battle between officers and enlisted. He had to get back to talk to Pete and convince him to take the medal and shut up. Nurse Jamison might tell someone that Pete was planning to make a fight of it to get back at the Captain. He said "Nurse, sir, we were just tossing the bull. No one is going to do any fragging."

"Corporal, there's something fishy going on here. They have put that man in isolation, there's talk about evacuating him out, and I know he told you something about fragging. Is he planning to kill himself?"

"No. He's fine." Jeff could tell that Nurse Jamison was sincerely concerned. He decided that he had to trust someone. He looked down at the stump that used to be one of his hard running legs and realized that he couldn't even sneak down to the end of the ward without help. "Pete didn't do it. He's being framed for what some officer did." Jeff went on to tell Nurse Jamison about the firefight and the medal and the cover up for the Captain.

She looked at him in disbelief. "How could anyone make up an accusation like that and hope to make it stick? He probably made up that story to save his skin."

"He didn't make up any stories. His lawyer told him what was going on. Before that, Pete was ready to accept whatever they told him."

"What about the fragging?"

"I don't know anything for sure, but I know officers. And if Pete is going to blow the whistle on an officer, he isn't going home first class. He's going in an aluminum box."

"Oh, dear Lord. You can't believe that. This has got to be stopped."

"Look Nurse. I trusted you because I thought you cared about your patients, but if you say anything you'll get Pete killed. And you and I would be on the same list."

"This isn't the mafia, Corporal. I can go to Colonel MacGill and tell him about this and the whole thing will be out in the open and cleared up before tomorrow."

"I don't know who the hell Colonel MacGill is, but I wouldn't be surprised to see his name on Pete's citation when he gets his Bronze Star."

Nurse Jamison's eyes flashed and for a moment Jeff thought she was going to hit him. She turned and marched down the ward to Pete's bedside and asked him if what Jeff had told her was true. Pete told her that it was and that he intended to counter charge the Captain with the same offense he had been accused of. She took his good hand and squeezed it. "You're going to need some high powered friends, Marine. I can help if you'll let me."

Jeff rolled up in his wheel chair and told Pete to keep his mouth shut. About that time the lawyer assigned to Pete's case walked in and just about had a fit. "I said this man was in isolation. He isn't supposed to talk to anyone."

Nurse Jamison explained what she had heard and what she proposed to do. The lawyer gave her almost the same argument that Jeff had except that he didn't think anyone would try to assassinate Pete if he didn't go along. He felt that Pete would be sent home, discharged, and forgotten about. Jeff said that he thought the lawyer had his head up his ass and locked. He realized that he had just insulted an officer, but it was too late to stop now. "If the brass is going from a desertion charge to a Bronze Star you can bet someone's butt is hanging way out. I say the only way Pete is going to get out of here alive is to go along and keep his mouth shut."

Pete finally broke in. "This is my fight and I intend to go all the way with it." He asked the lawyer "How do I charge an officer with desertion?"

"I don't think you are going to get the chance. What I came here to tell you is that you're on your way out. The charges have been dropped, your medals are being forwarded to Tokyo and you'll be on a plane in less than an hour." He handed Nurse Jamison a packet and indicated that it contained transfer orders to be acted on immediately.

Nurse Jamison wheeled Jeff back up the ward while Pete and his lawyer argued at the far end. A few minutes later two orderlies and two M.P.s moved Pete to a stretcher and carried him out to a waiting ambulance. Jeff watched in silence as they went out the back door. He didn't even know Pete's last name. He vowed to get the name and an address so he could follow up on whether or not Pete made it home.

CHAPTER 14

Ellie Karpaski had been true to her word. She drank two strong scotches with water and then two more without water. Tony did his best to get a meal on the table for the kids and he set a place at the table for Ellie. She composed herself for the sake of the children and joined them at the table. She insisted on wine with dinner. "The good stuff, Tony. Not that camel piss with the screw top bottle." The kids naturally thought that was the funniest thing they had ever heard and Tony knew that by noon tomorrow all the kids in the neighborhood would be yelling "camel piss" at each other.

"The damage is done" thought Tony. "You kids finish up and you can watch the Disney movie. If you're nice to each other I'll bring you some ice cream." They bolted down the rest of the hamburger on their plates and ran for the living room to fight over who got to control the T.V. set. "Remember to be nice", Tony called after them to no avail.

Ellie finished off the bottle of wine and true to her nature she got sloppier and funnier as the drinks took effect. She knew her limitations and generally stopped at two drinks unless the occasion demanded otherwise. Tony managed to get her to eat some dinner but only after he promised to break open a bottle of champagne. They kept a bottle or two on hand for unexpected occasions and tonight qualified in Ellie's mind. "Grog for the crew, Cap'n", she slurred. "Splice the rain mace, sailor."

"I think it's 'splice the main brace', honey."

"Right, slice the grace place. I can talk navy with the best of 'em. A toast: To the detail officers of the navy. Those sons of bitches that write our husband's orders and send them off the fuck knows where." Ellie drained her glass threw it across the room at the wall. "Oh crap," mumbled Ellie as the glass shattered, "we're supposed to do that with the slicing brandy glasses, not the slicing champagne glasses. Get me some brandy, Tony. We have to do the whole thing over again or it doesn't count."

Tony checked on the kids in the living room. They were blissfully unaware of the crashing crystal. "Are you sure you want more?" Ellie was glaring at him and pointing to the kitchen where the liquor was stored. Tony knew it was useless to protest. He went out to the kitchen, but before he came back in he helped himself to a solid slug of the brandy. He knew he had the duty with the kids, but he really needed a drink. Besides, this wouldn't last much longer. Ellie had good short-term capacity, but no staying power when it came to drinking.

Tony was up early the next morning. He shaved and dressed in working khakis and got the kids fed and off to school with time to spare. He knew that Ellie wasn't going to be as much fun this morning as she was last night. She had proposed three more toasts, told a couple of raunchy jokes, and was on the phone trying to get the Chief of Naval Personnel's home phone number when she slipped into oblivion. Tony had gotten her up to bed and undressed before she started to feel sick. He eased her into the bathroom and prudently closed the door until things quieted down. Then he washed her hands and face and led her back to bed. He knew she would sleep through until morning.

Tony wrote a short note to Ellie assuring her that all of her actions the night before had been contained within the walls of their house. He let her know that he had gotten the kids to bed before she passed out and they were satisfied with this morning's explanation that she had an upset stomach and wanted to sleep late. They were off to school by the time she woke up. Ellie went to great lengths never to embarrass herself or her family. It was one of the reasons that she rarely drank liquor -- she needed to know that she was doing the right thing and the booze robbed her of that precious asset.

Tony was heading out the door when the phone rang. He ran to get it before it woke Ellie. She couldn't let a phone ring without being answered immediately. It was Parker. "We have a call from COM 12, Skipper. They want you to call them back ASAP. Something about your orders."

"Parker, this better not be one of your off-balance attempts at humor. I'm not in the mood."

"If it's a joke, I'm not in on it. Captain Kraushauf himself was on the phone. He said they're moving your orders up."

"Oh, shit!" said Tony. "I'm on my way in. If he calls again tell him you just missed me at home and that I'm on the way." As Tony bolted out the door to his car, Ellie quietly replaced the extension phone receiver.

Tony got on the phone as soon as he reached his desk. Parker eased into the C.O.'s office and closed the door behind him. Tony motioned for him to take a seat. Headquarters put the call through to Captain Kraushauf immediately. Once Tony identified himself, all Parker heard was "Yes, sir; yes, sir; yes, sir. I'll be here Captain, thank you."

Parker slumped in his chair. "No Joke, huh, Skipper?"

"The TET Offensive created a few job openings. They want to get me into school in Coronado for the next class instead of catching the one I was scheduled for two months down the line. I have five days to turn over the Command. They're sending a temporary relief from COM 12. He's on the way."

"Did he say who they're sending?"

"Lieutenant Stein. Your favorite inspection officer."

"Aw, tell me you're pulling my leg, Skipper. I can't work for that prick."

"There are those who will defend to the death your right to say that, Yeoman Parker, but if you want to hang on to your stripes you better start thinking positively about the good lieutenant. Now drag your sorry ass out of that chair and get my turnover file in here. I want this change of command to start the minute Stein hits the property line."

Parker passed the word to the rest of the troops and the Chief of the Center called for a Field Day immediately. Brooms, swabs, and lawn mowers were in action in less than five minutes. When Lieutenant Stein arrived two hours later the Center was sparkling. Records were laid out for inspection. All hands were in dress blues and assembled in the drill hall standing at parade rest. Sailors could drag their feet getting ready for an inspection. It was in tribute to Cdr. Karpaski, the best C.O. they ever worked for, that preparations were made in record time. The Chief reported to Cdr. Karpaski that the men were awaiting his orders.

Tony had noticed the action around the Center with satisfaction. When he saw the Chief in front of the building in dress blues he realized that his men were going an extra mile to make things look perfect. He quickly shifted into his own dress uniform.

When the Chief knocked on the office door, Tony was offering his relief the traditional cup of coffee. "Ready for inspection, sir," reported the Chief. Lt. Stein appeared a bit uncomfortable in his working khaki uniform slightly rumpled from the drive down from San Francisco. Tony knew how his men had suffered under Lt. Stein during the last Headquarters inspection and he figured they deserved a shot at the little martinet who always demanded results about two grades above perfection during inspections. "Thank you, Chief. Lt. Stein and I will start the turnover procedure with a review of the troops immediately. I'll let you know the rest of the day's itinerary right after that."

"Commander, I haven't had a chance to prepare to conduct an inspection."

"Nonsense, Lieutenant. You yourself said at our last inspection that a good navy man is always ready for inspection. Please follow me and we'll get this show on the road."

Before Lt. Stein could protest further, Karpaski was out the door and heading for the drill hall. Stein rubbed his shoe tops on the back of his trousers and straightened his tie. He tried unsuccessfully to smooth out the wrinkles in his uniform as he followed Karpaski up the passageway.

The station staff snapped to attention with a single click of their collective heels when the Chief announced "Attention on deck."

Tony was bursting with pride. His men could have stood honor guard for the President. Shoes sparkled, white hats gleamed, backs were straight, eyes were riveted straight ahead.

There wasn't a button out of line. Not the smallest piece of lint on the neatly pressed uniforms. Tony walked ahead with Lt. Stein two steps behind. He stopped in front of each man and eyed him head to toe and back again, and then with a curt nod of his head he moved to the next man. After inspecting the last man he marched briskly to the front and ordered the Chief to dismiss the troops and have them assemble in the Rec Room to await further orders. He made no mention of the outstanding presentation the men had made. He knew they would want him to treat it as an everyday occurrence for Lt. Stein's benefit. The Chief snapped to attention and rendered a perfect salute. "Aye, aye, sir!"

Tony marched out without further word or any indication that he cared whether Stein followed him or not. When they got back to the office Tony handed his relief the turn-over file and said that he would inform the men of the order for records and equipment inspections. "I'll give you a tour of the Center right after lunch. I thought it would be well if you had a chance to meet with the men and see if there were any immediate questions that came to mind."

Lt. Stein finally stopped gaping and found his voice. "Commander, we have five days to complete this turn-over. Do we have to do everything this morning?"

"You have five days, Lieutenant. I'm scheduling a change of command ceremony for 1600 tomorrow whether you're ready or not. Then I'm going to spend as much time with my wife and family as I can before I have to leave. I'll give the Chief his orders on the way out and he'll introduce you around. I'm going home to tell my wife about this big fucking surprise. I'll see you at 1300 for a building tour. If you have any questions, ask the Chief. As you well know, he is the Executive Officer of this command."

CHAPTER 15

It was close to midnight when Nurse Jamison pushed Jeff's wheelchair out into the paved area located between the hospital ward and the hill that sloped down to the perimeter fence.

"I hope I'm not keeping you up past your bedtime, but I had to talk to you alone."

"Your wish is my command, Nurse, sir."

"This isn't funny, Corporal. I talked to Colonel MacGill. He had no idea what was going on with Pete and his Captain."

"Jesus Christ, Jamison, tell me you didn't really talk to the Colonel." Jeff had gotten so excited at the prospect of the brass having to bring Pete's case out in the open that he stood up on his one good leg and had to hop around to keep his balance.

Nurse Jamison went to help Jeff and he fell into her outstretched arms and they both fell to the ground, Jeff half on top of the nurse. For a moment neither of them moved, then Jeff realized that he was nose to nose with a very beautiful woman. On an impulse he kissed her. She kissed him back and for a brief instant neither of them thought of anything but the passion of the moment. As they rolled over and Nurse Jamison moved her body on top of Jeff he banged his bad leg against the wheelchair and he recoiled in pain. She realized what had happened and became a nurse again immediately. Her arms cradled Jeff and her gentle hands stroked his sweating brow. "Are you o.k? Wow, that was a moment to remember."

"I'm fine. Damned leg. I never expected to have a chance with you and when I do get a chance I screw it up because of this stupid stump."

"It's a good thing it happened. I'm a professional, Corporal. I have no business rolling around on the ground in the middle of the night with patients. Even sweeties like you."

Jeff had completely forgotten what had been said that got him out of his chair in the first place. "Do you really think I'm a sweetie?"

"I've been here for eight months with nothing but men around me and you're the first one that's broken through the barrier. A woman could get in real trouble in a place like this. I think you're one of the most special men I've ever met."

"Does that mean that the barrier is still down? I don't mind a bit if you want to take advantage of me."

"The barrier is back up, and just in time. You're being shipped out tomorrow and I don't need any funny ideas cluttering up my brain."

"I'm leaving? I didn't see any orders."

"I held on to the list with you name on it until I could talk to you. Now stay in your chair, I want to tell you about Colonel MacGill. I told him about the incident with Pete, but I left your name out of it. In fact, he promised to leave me out of it. He's going to initiate an investigation. Pete will get his day in court, but it will be from a distance so he's safe."

"They shot him once, they may do it again."

"Not a chance. Once the investigation starts, the people involved will be too busy saving their skins to try to do any more damage. Besides, Pete will be stateside before things heat up."

"What are they going to do about the medals?"

"He'll get his Purple Heart for being wounded, but the Bronze Star has been killed. He's being treated as a witness so he knows that action is being taken against the Captain and the other officers. Any charges that come will be brought as a result of the investigation so there is no need for Pete to put his neck on the line. He has the best of both worlds."

"I'll believe it when I read about it in the papers. But thanks, anyway. You're a nice person Nurse, sir."

Nurse Jamison leaned over and gave Jeff a passionate kiss on the mouth. He reached up to hold her but she moved behind his chair and started wheeling him back to the ward. "You've got my address here at the hospital. Write to me and we'll make a date to have a wing-ding when I get back to the States." She wished she hadn't said that. She had joked with patients leaving for home before, agreeing to meet for a drink when they all got home, but this time she meant it. She was getting all misty over an enlisted man that was too young for her that she had known for only a matter of days.

"I've already written the letter. I'll mail it the minute I get back."

The next morning Jeff loaded on the bus with ten other walking wounded and headed for the airport. Nurse Jamison was nowhere in sight.

CHAPTER 16

Lieutenant Jack Walker's plane hit the runway at Travis Air Force Base at a sideways angle with a terrible thump and began fishtailing, brakes screeching. "Not again" thought Jack. "I'm an hour from home and the damned plane is going to crash." The pilot brought the Boeing 707 under control and announced over the P.A. System in a calm, deep voice: "Please excuse the bumpy landing, gentlemen. That was not what they taught us at Pan Am landing school. We'll be offloading in just a few minutes. Welcome home!" The cabin erupted with laughter and catcalls as 150 veterans realized that they had survived one more time.

For just about everyone else on the plane this was Day 366. They had served their 365 day tour of duty and were back in the world. Jack's situation was unusual. He was going to get a thirty day leave and he would be going back to finish his tour. The morning after his night on the town with Buck he had called his command and spoke with LCDR Hilgo. Commander Parks had been badly wounded in a rocket attack and Hilgo was acting C.O.

Jack's first thought was that Hilgo would probably cancel his orders home and put him back to work. But he got a real surprise from the prissy so-and-so. "I can't see where you can be of any use around here for the next month or so. I talked to COMNAVFORV (Commander Naval Forces Viet Nam) yesterday and they're changing your orders to leave directly from Saigon back to the States. If you can find your way over to Headquarters, your orders are waiting for you."

"Wow!. I don't know what to say, skipper."

"I don't expect you to say anything. Get your ass on that plane and give your wife a kiss for me."

Hilgo was so out of character that Jack forgot to ask about Commander Parks and the rest of the crew. He just stammered his thanks, hung up, packed his bag and called for a car.

The plane taxied up to the loading ramp thirty-six hours after departing Tan Son Nhut. They had stopped briefly in Japan and again in Alaska, but most of the time they had been in the air. Jack was a little stiff from sitting so long but he took advantage of being the third person off the plane and managed to be the first man to the telephones in the waiting room.

Sally let out whoop when she heard Jack's voice on the phone. "Where are you? Fairfield? Sit tight, we'll be there in an hour. I love you!"

Jack stood looking into the dead phone in his hand. Sally hadn't even said good-bye. "She hasn't changed a bit" he mused to himself. "She's probably half way here already."

Jack was standing in front of the terminal with his bag at his feet when he heard the siren. Two sirens. One was a California Highway Patrol car and the other was a Military Police jeep. The two were being led by a dusty station wagon that skidded to a halt right in front of Jack. A very pregnant woman muscled her way out of the front seat, took a small boy from the car and ran to him. Jack was too dumbfounded to talk. He held Sally and Todd and laughed.

The Military Policeman had to tap Sally on the shoulder to get her attention. "Ma'm, you went through the main gate without stopping for identification."

Sally leveled her best stare at the young M.P. and said "That's not true. I did stop." She turned her attention back to Jack. "Pull rank or something, honey. Make him go away."

The highway patrolman sized up the situation and asked the M.P. to step over to his car and talk to him for a moment. "Let's just let this one go. I clocked her at 85 on the freeway, but I sure as hell don't want my picture in the paper giving a ticket to a pregnant woman with a toddler greeting her husband home from the war."

The M.P. wasn't the brightest guy in the world. He wanted to arrest Sally, but his partner joined in and convinced him that no real harm had been done. The M.P. finally agreed, but not without swaggering over to Sally and telling her it had better not happen again.

"It will never happen again. From now on my husband does the driving." Jack and Sally went home.

★ ★ ★

The hospital in Japan was nothing like the one in Da Nang. Jeff found himself back in a traditional military setting. Doctors and nurses wore proper uniforms. Personnel were addressed by rank. Everything was spit and polish. There were what seemed like hundreds of Japanese nurse's aides padding around and performing every task that needed attention with an immediacy and efficiency that was amazing. It was clean and Jeff was well cared for, but there was no Nurse Jamison to brighten his day. He knew it was silly to be thinking of her. She was an officer, she was older. That last night in Da Nang was a fluke. Just one of those things that happens and everyone forgets about. It didn't mean a thing...like hell it didn't! He couldn't keep his mind off of her.

For two days Jeff just laid in his bed and watched the comings and goings of the staff. Red Cross volunteers brought him cookies, stationery to write letters and just sat and talked with him. He began to wonder if this was where he was going to spend the rest of his life. On the morning of the third day he became the center of attention. He was whisked off for X-Rays, then to the lab for blood and urine tests. Three different doctors looked at his leg. Then he went to see the psychiatrist.

"How do you feel?"

"I feel fine."

"Are you looking forward to going home?"

"Naturally."

"No problems about you leg?"

"I wish to hell it was still there."

"Who do you blame for losing your leg?"

"Charlie, I guess. He laid out the punji stake."

" How do you feel about that?"

"Excuse me, Doctor, but I don't have a problem. I wish to hell that I was going home in one piece, but that ain't the way it is. I've thought about it and after seeing what happened to some of the other guys in the hospital, I'm not so bad off."

"I'm glad to hear you have given it some thought. That's what I was going to suggest you do. Right now, you're in your own environment. As you said, some are far worse off than you. But when you go home you're going to be surrounded by a different group of people, most of whom haven't gone through what you have. In fact, some of them will be rooting for the people who did this to you."

"I don't think so. Not in my hometown. I'll be fine."

The doctor stood up and walked over to Jeff's wheelchair and held out his hand to shake. "Good luck, young fellow." He pressed a buzzer on his desk and a Japanese orderly came in to wheel Jeff back to his bed.

The next few days passed slowly and without any fanfare. On the morning of the seventh day a navy commander, a marine first lieutenant, and a yeoman came through the ward and stopped briefly at each bed and presented the occupant with a Purple Heart Medal. At one bed several down from Jeff's a doctor and two nurses joined the commander and Jeff could hear the yeoman call out "Attention to Orders". Then the commander read a citation and presented the man with a second medal.

It was a surprise when they got to Jeff's bed and the yeoman called out "Attention to Orders and the presentation of the Silver Star Award for Gallantry in Action to Corporal Geoffery Paul Dunlay, United States Marine Corps".

The citation was quite long and detailed. It explained how Jeff and two other men assaulted an enemy mortar emplacement and a detachment of superior enemy forces at absolute risk of their lives, and that when both of his subordinates were killed by enemy fire "Corporal Dunlay, with total disregard for his own safety, pressed his attack on the enemy emplacement thereby disrupting their mortar attack on his platoon, giving the platoon time to withdraw, regroup, and provide aid to twenty-two casualties. Additional casualties would have been certainly inflicted had it not been for the immediate and persistent pressure placed on the enemy by Corporal Dunaly's detachment." It went on to explain how his selfless actions led to him being seriously wounded and captured by the enemy.

The commander and the yeoman stood at attention as the marine lieutenant pinned the Silver Star on Jeff's blue pajama top and then presented him with his Purple Heart. One would think that that was enough excitement for one day, but there was more to come. The commander interrupted the congratulations by calling "Attention to Orders" and he proceeded to read the citation for the Bronze Star with Combat V being awarded to Jeff for his subsequent escape and evasion from the enemy, which led to his freedom the rescue of a fellow prisoner.

The commander shook Jeff's hand and then stepped back and joined in the applause that erupted from the beds up and down the ward. Jeff's eyes were filled with tears as he looked at the men who cheered him. For the most part they had suffered wounds worse than his and they were all heroes just for being where they were. Yet they smiled and cheered him and poured out an affection that only comrades bloodied in war can share. The presentation party had completed its mission and left the ward. One by one the wounded in the ward came over to Jeff's bed and shook his hand. They fingered the medals and carried them down to show to the men who couldn't leave their beds. Jeff was so choked up he could hardly talk.

The psychiatrist stood at the far end of the ward and gazed dejectedly at the scene before him. One of the nurses came up and punched him playfully on the arm. "Why so glum, Doc, don't you think he deserves the medals?"

"It's not that. Right now he's a hero among heroes. He's getting the best medicine that anyone can provide, the honest admiration of his peers. But sometime, I don't know when, he's going to be alone and the price that was paid for those medals is going to come home to him. It will tear him apart. I just hope he's tough enough to be a hero."

Later that afternoon the orderlies came through the ward and helped a select group gather their belongings. They transferred them to wheelchairs and moved them out of the ward. Jeff was among the men starting the final leg of the journey back to the world.

CHAPTER 17

Jack and Sally were busy catching up on all the things that had been happening to each other. Jack was trying to get to know Todd, but it was difficult. The little fellow was wary of him and Jack couldn't react in the spontaneous way of a parent the way Sally did. She had been a parent all these months, but Jack had been out of the picture. He didn't know the little songs to sing, the games to play, the proper way to help feed or bathe a child. He had a sudden fearful thought. What if he had been killed? What if he had not come back? He had missed so much as it was, and the navy being what it is, he would miss more. He had known hundreds of officers and enlisted men and they all faced this same problem. Many of them prided themselves on the fact that they spent most of their married lives away from home. They joked with expressions like 'If the navy had wanted you to have a wife and kids, they would have issued them to you in boot camp.' Or the old salts would say, "Sailors belong on ships and ships belong at sea." Jack didn't want to leave his family again. It wasn't right.

"Sally, what would you say if I wanted to leave the navy?"

"Is this a serious question, or are you just testing me?"

"I'm dead serious. Being back here with you and the baby makes me realize what I almost lost."

"My first reaction is, I'd say you finally came to your senses. I told you when we got married that I would go along with anything you wanted to do. I knew what I was getting into. But if you wanted to get out and do something civilized, I'd be the happiest woman alive."

"There was a time when I thought there was nothing in the world I would ever want to do except be a naval officer and someday become an admiral. Now that I've said the words about giving it up out loud I think I've been on the wrong track all along."

"You're really serious about this, aren't you?"

"I started thinking about it on the plane on the way back. Even before that, I guess. Before I got captured we had some bull sessions sitting around the camp. Most of us were coming to the conclusion that the war was wrong. Not just this war, but the whole idea of our going into a foreign country and killing the people we said we were there to help."

"Sounds like you got some first class communist indoctrination in that jungle."

Jack looked startled. "Do you suppose that's what happened to me?"

"I doubt it, but something has gotten under your skin."

"You know what it was? The uniform thing. That's what did it."

"What in the world is the 'uniform thing'?"

"When we were getting ready to come back, I was told to shift into civilian clothes for the flight. I had to go out and buy a shirt and some pants before I could get on the plane."

"I wondered where you got that ugly outfit. I almost didn't recognize you at the airport."

"That's what did it. I went over there all full of piss and vinegar, waving the flag and thinking I was doing right by my country and my navy. I damned near got killed and when it's time to come back they tell me to put my uniform in a sack and keep it out of sight."

"Did they really say that?"

"Just about. I asked what the reason was for going home in civvies and they told me that there was some anti-war sentiment back in States and the government didn't want people to know how many troops were moving in and out of the country. Most of the guys on then plane were getting on busses and going straight to San Francisco International for flights home. They didn't want them recognized as Viet Nam Vets. How's that for a crock?"

Sally thought about the phone calls calling Jack a killer, and all the riots and protests on the college campuses and the news on the T.V. every night. Some nights the war and the protests got equal coverage. It was like a war within a war. She felt pretty sure in her own mind that if things had been different she would have been out protesting the war. It just didn't seem like a good idea for a pregnant woman with a husband in Viet Nam to do. She smiled at Jack. "I'm not going to turn in my dependent I.D. card just yet. When you get back with your navy buddies you'll probably forget all about this getting out business."

"You may be right, but we've got to talk about it some more."

During the conversation, Todd had crawled up on Jack's lap and nodded off to sleep in his arms. He sat looking at his son for a long time. Sally didn't say anything, she just watched the two of them. It was something she had been dreaming about for months. The phone rang and brought them all back to reality. It was Tony Karpaski calling to tell Sally that his orders had been changed and that he was leaving. Lt. Stein would be taking over her file. He was delighted to hear that Jack had made it back and that they could close out the CACO file. Sally and Tony had become what passed for good friends under the circumstances. They could talk together easily. Sally asked if he could come over and meet Jack. "In fact", said Sally "why don't you bring your wife and we'll make a party out of it." Then she saw the look on Jack's face and realized that she had gotten so in the habit of making decisions on her own that she had forgotten that he should have been consulted. "Hang on a minute, Tony." She explained to Jack who was on the phone and apologized for going off making plans without asking him.

"Good grief, yes." said Jack. "Tell him to get on over here. I owe that guy more than he will ever know for looking out for you and Todd."

"Tony, Jack says get on over here."

Tony had tried to get her attention before she went off the line. "I don't think I can make it, and strictly between you and me, I'm not sure this would be a good time to suggest it to Ellie. We only have four more days and I have to leave."

Sally could hear the torment in Tony's voice and she knew that he and Ellie were having a hard time over the sudden change of orders. "I understand. It's not a good time for you. But the invitation is open. You have our number and if you get a spare minute give a call. You can come here or we'll meet you on neutral ground. God bless you, Karpaski."

Sally was about to hang up when Jack started waving his arms. "Don't hang up, I want to talk to him."

Sally told Tony to hang on for a minute. She handed the phone to Jack and took Todd and left the room. Whatever Jack had to say would probably be better said without his wife standing there crying.

Jack and Tony talked for almost 15 minutes. At first the conversation was an outpouring of appreciation from Jack and congratulations from Tony, but then the business of war took over. The two officers compared notes and Jack gave Tony some advice on what to expect in Viet Nam. Tony had a hundred questions, but what he really wanted to know was if he was going to get back alive. No one on earth could answer that question so he didn't ask. Jack could sense that Tony was struggling. He remembered his own feelings and doubts after his orders came and he knew he was heading for a war. The conversation finally deteriorated the way they do when the subject matter is limited and the two parties can't think of anything more to say. Jack felt awkward, but he said, "I owe you, fella. Keep in touch. And if your wife needs anything while you're gone, tell her to call me. Anytime. If I'm here and I can help, all she has to do is ask." Tony thanked him and they both mumbled goodbyes.

Maybe their paths would cross again, thought Jack. The navy had a way of bringing people together as well as separating them. Sally came back into the room and found Jack with a far away look in his eyes. "An old sailor once told me to watch out for the guys with the 'two-thousand yard stare'. You look like the weight of the world is on your back."

Jack was reliving events of the recent past. Talking to Tony about Viet Nam brought back a jumble of memories and they ended centering on the hut in the jungle with the interrogator hammering away with his questions and his insinuations. It was a frightening experience and might have gone on longer if Sally hadn't spoken. As it was, it took Jack a few counts to get back to reality. He tried to make light of it, but Sally could tell that, for that moment at least, Jack had a problem.

Jack stood up and walked over and gave Sally a kiss on the cheek. "I think it's just about the cocktail hour. What can I get you, honey?"

"It's straight orange juice for me until our daughter arrives."

"Right. Orange juice for two, coming up."

"Don't be silly. Fix yourself a stiff belt. You're not pregnant. Besides, I want to have something to hold over you when the going gets tough."

Jack was going to insist again when the phone rang. "I'll get it, maybe Tony thought of something else he needed." Jack answered the phone and quickly passed it to Sally. "Someone named Suzie for you."

Sally took the receiver and held her hand over the mouthpiece, "I haven't had a chance to tell you about Suzie. You're going to love her."

Jack could tell from the way Sally was talking that this was someone she really liked, someone she was in sync with. Sally let out a whoop and was bubbling over with excitement. "He's home? I can't believe it. When did he get here?" She went off again making more plans without asking Jack. He could tell that they were going to have company whether he wanted it or not.

Todd was back up on Jack's lap playing a game of hiding behind his fingers and giggling when Jack said he couldn't see him. Sally finally got off the phone and told Jack that Suzie was coming over with her big brother. She explained how the two of them had met and what a comfort it was to have someone to talk to who understood what was happening. Sally's greatest complement to anyone was that "they understood" what she was talking about. Jack had no idea that Sally knew someone who had a relative who was a prisoner of war, much less someone who had managed to escape. For a moment he thought "What if it turned out to be that corporal from the hut?" but he quickly dismissed that possibility as something out of the Twilight Zone.

Jack volunteered to do the diaper duty and get Todd off to bed. Sally had taken care of giving him a bath earlier. He was busy tucking Todd in and playing the bedtime games as best he could. All Jack could do was imitate what he had seen Sally do the night before, but he was getting the hang of it. Todd was finally wearing down when the visitors arrived. Sally called from the living room for Jack to hurry and come out and meet Suzie and her brother. It took him a few more minutes to get Todd settled down. When he entered the living room Sally was standing with an attractive young girl and they were both talking to the man in the marine corps uniform sitting with his back to Jack. The man's leg was propped up on an ottoman and his crutches were wedged into the chair next to him.

"Jack, this is my friend Suzie that I told you about, and this handsome young fellow is her brother, Jeff."

Jeff half turned in his chair to say hello as Jack came around to shake hands. Jack's hand fell to his side and he looked dumbfounded. Jeff looked like someone had just introduced him to the Pope and he wasn't sure what to do next. No one said a word. The two women could tell that something extraordinary was happening. All four of them came to the realization at the same time and they were hugging, and crying and saying that this couldn't be happening.

When the pandemonium died down, Jack was the first to speak. "I was waiting for my boss to send your address so I could make contact. I owe you my life. Where the hell did you come from?"

Jeff had gotten up on his good leg, but he decided it would be safer to get back into his chair. "My sister told me about a friend who had a husband who had been captured, but I never thought it would be you."

"This has to be the coincidence of all time." said Jack. "If it weren't for this guy getting me out, God knows where I'd be right now. He got away when I was out cold."

"I tried to wake you up!"

"Oh, hell. At first I thought you took off on me, but when I realized how tired I was I knew that you couldn't wake me up. Probably the best thing for both of us. I never could have done what you did. They had to carry me out."

Jack and Jeff recounted the escape story. The women had a thousand questions and the four of them babbled on for an hour telling each other all the coincidences that brought them together. They all agreed it was one in a million.

Everyone had avoided talking about Jeff's leg. Finally, Jack had to ask. "How did you make it out on one leg?"

"I had two legs for the walk out. When I got to the hospital they tried to save it, but between the punji stake and the infection that set in they had to take it off. It was just one of those things."

"Jesus" thought Jack. What does he mean: one of those things. "Will you get an artificial leg?"

"Oh, yeah. I'm just here for a 48-hour pass. I have to report back to the hospital tomorrow night. They said I would be in rehab for a couple of months. I can kiss the football scholarships goodbye, but I'll be able to move around like normal when they get through with me."

Jack brought out a round of drinks and they sat talking for a long time. Suzie was sitting on the arm of Jeff's chair with her arm around him. Jack and Sally were sitting on the couch facing them. The conversation died and each of the four sat silently with his and her own thoughts. Sally held Jack's hand up to her cheek, then she kissed it and nestled her head on his shoulder. Jeff worked his crutches out of the chair and got to his feet. Suzie joined him. There were silent hugs all around and short plans for a big family reunion dinner as soon as Jeff got his next pass.

After Suzie and Jeff departed, Jack said, "That's a man the world is going to hear from."

CHAPTER 18

The homecoming had been hectic for Jeff. There was an awkwardness when he was talking to his father. His mother hardly stopped crying, and brother Les was acting strangely. He had no idea what had gone on in his family while he was overseas, but the people he had known and loved had changed. Only Suzie acted like a normal person. They were all interested in his medals and the family knew better than anyone else what the loss of Jeff's leg meant to him. Sports, especially football, had been his life. Jeff had known he would never make it to the pros, but he expected to get a college scholarship. Now that was a lost hope. It's normal for people to ask 'What are you going to do when you get out of the marines?' Everyone he met asked the same questions, but he didn't have any answers. He had been glad for the diversion Suzie set up to bring him over to meet Jack and Sally. He had been able to talk to them as he had with the people in the hospital; they understood his experience in Viet Nam. There was a common bond and conversations didn't get hung up because someone was afraid to say the wrong thing. Everyone knew the score. Not so with the civilians. They couldn't get past the medals and the missing leg. Jeff was almost happy to get back to the hospital.

Rehabilitation for someone who has lost a leg is a long, but steady, process. First the leg has to heal. The patient gets out of his wheelchair and moves around on crutches. Balance and mobility return. Then comes the prosthesis, often referred to as a wooden leg.

Learning to make the darned thing work like a real leg is a bit easier when the knee isn't involved. But there is still the uncertainty of a mechanical ankle. Jeff's natural athletic ability with strength, agility, and balance built in would make the transition easier.

Jeff phoned home to see how things were going. His brother, Les, answered the phone.

"Hey, big brother, from what you say you're moving pretty good. When do you get some time off?"

"As a matter of fact, I'm getting a week-end pass starting Friday. Do you think you could drive over and pick me up, Les?"

"It's the least I can do in return for the use of your truck all these months. I've been keeping it in good shape for you."

"I won't be driving for a while. Still a little slow on the response. Anyway, I want to get a car. Something the ladies will appreciate. The truck is half yours anyway. Bill says you bought him out."

"He said he needed the money and he was away at school. You don't mind, do you?"

"As a matter of fact, why don't we just call it even. You give me a couple of rides until I get my leg in shape and you keep the truck."

Les was flustered by the gift. Jeff had always been generous with him, but giving him a truck was too much. The younger brother wanted to do something in return. Show he was worthy.

"How about coming over to the Cal campus with me Friday. I know a few girls over there. We could bum around and see what's what."

"You're going to fix your big brother up with some college girl? Since when have you been going to college?"

"I went over there a few times, made some friends. Can you go? We could just stop by on the way home. We wouldn't have to stay."

"Sure, why not. I've been thinking about school. Maybe I could pick up some info about enrolling."

★ ★ ★

Jack and Sally fell into their old routines of married life. At times it seemed like he had never been away. He was becoming more adept at handling the baby, even spending time alone with him while Sally went shopping. It wasn't all roses. Sally's independent nature made it difficult for her to remember to check with Jack before dashing off to each new activity. Tony Karpaski called and said that he and Ellie wanted to get together for dinner. Time was short. He had only two days left before leaving for training. Sally suggested a restaurant, the time, and that evening for dinner. She was arranging a baby sitter and laying out a dress when Jack came in from some chores outside. She told Jack the news. He tried to look pleased, but there was no enthusiasm.

"What's the trouble, sailor? Not up to a night on the town?"

"I've been thinking about a quiet evening at home all morning. I'm feeling a bit weary. Guess I just have the blahs. Maybe a night out will cure what ails me."

"If I've gone over the line again, tell me."

"That's not it. I've been wrestling with this business of getting out of the navy. I need to talk to you. I need some time. For some reason, I'm scared as hell."

"Scared about what?"

"I don't know. It's like I want to run and hide."

"Is it from being a prisoner?"

"Could be. The shrink told me to expect some flashbacks and nervousness. But I haven't even thought about that. You've been the cure I needed. I look at Todd and wonder what I'm doing for him. I think about our future and I just get scared."

"I better call Tony and tell him we need to back out."

"No, please. Don't do that. We owe him. And I want to meet his wife. I told Tony that I'd be there for her. I'll be o.k. Whoops. I smell something interesting here." Jack picked Todd up and carried him off to the bathroom to change his diaper. Sally watched them disappear around the corner; she bit her lip and fidgeted around the room for a while, thinking.

Jack was finishing a masterful job of diaper changing when Sally came up behind him and put her arms around his chest. She snuggled her lips into his neck and said "Hang in there, sailor. In a couple of months I'll have my figure back and you'll get some lovin' that will make all the ghosts go away."

As her strength and love flowed into him, Jack felt the despair and panic melting away. "If you ever stop loving me, just take a gun and shoot me. I need you Mrs. Walker."

The evening with the Karpaskis went beautifully. They had a corner table at a noisy restaurant with good food and funny waiters. Birthday and anniversary parties at other tables brought the waiters together in surprisingly good quartets. Cheap red wine was opened with a flourish, and mocking noises, like champagne being opened. The owner of the place was an aspiring entertainer who never quite made the big time, but played one hell of a ragtime piano. Something was going on all the time to keep the crowd amused. Everyone at the table did his and her share to keep things light and happy. Jack and Tony traded sea stories while their wives ragged at them for being big, macho military poops.

Tony had wished that he could spend some time alone talking to Jack. He wanted to know what to expect. What was it like going to war? Should he be doing anything to prepare himself? What could he do to make it easier on Ellie? A million questions, and really, no one had the answers. It was different for everyone. Jack had a fleeting memory of the new officer who reported to the Squadron. His first night in he bunked with Jack until another room could be set up. In the middle of the night Jack heard a scream and looked over to see the new fellow literally climbing the wall trying to escape something in his nightmare. Jack pretended to sleep through it and never mentioned the incident. The new officer turned out to be a good Swift Boat Commander, but no amount of guidance could have prepared him for his first night in Da Nang when he was alone with his dreams. What worked for one might be a disaster for another. Regardless, the chance for Jack and Tony to talk alone never developed, probably for the better.

The evening ended with hugs and promises all around to keep in touch, to write, to call if anyone needed anything. Ellie wasn't sure, but she may go back east after Tony left. Her family was there, familiar surroundings and all that. They exchanged addresses and the couples drove off in two different directions, each with the premonition that they would never see the other again. It was a quiet sadness that people touched by war come to grips with.

★ ★ ★

It was the same day that Jeff had his first brush with college life. After picking Jeff up at the hospital, Les headed straight to the old building that housed the infamous "Thirteen". Les went up the dark stairway first and Jeff maneuvered his crutches easily taking the risers two at a time. The Senator was dozing on the old sofa against the wall. When he saw Jeff's clean features and close-cropped hair, he was sure it was a police raid. He rolled off the sofa into a crouch and his eyes darted from the door to the window looking for an escape route. Les didn't understand what the Senator's problem was -- nor did the Senator, actually -- and he casually introduced his brother, not even paying attention to the ridiculous posture his odd friend was presenting.

"Brother? It never occurred to me that you had a family." Still wary of Jeff's appearance, the Senator looked him up and down suspiciously, and then resumed his place on the couch without even saying hello.

Jeff started to move over to shake hands but stopped when he saw that the Senator wasn't interested. "So this is where my little brother spends his spare time. What is this place, some kind of hideout?"

Les was embarrassed by the reception Jeff had gotten. He tried to make light of it. "Yeah. This is where the Thirteen meet to conquer the world."

"You mean there is another dozen characters yet to come?"

"Actually only seven or eight. I call myself the thirteenth member. Sounds evil."

Jeff got the uneasy feeling that his was back in Da Nang at one of those badly lighted bars that served everything from booze to drugs to women. They were happy to relieve you of your money or anything else you owned. It was the kind of place that you got drunk before you visited, and stayed drunk to forget where you were.

"What's going on Les? This place looks like bad news to me. Not to mention the inhabitants."

"Fuck you, soldier." The Senator didn't like Jeff's looks and he wanted him out of there.

Les started to protest, but Jeff was way ahead of him. "I'm not a soldier, I'm a Marine you asshole. If you have something to say to me get you skinny ass off that sofa and come over here and say it."

"Take it easy, big tough brother. I'm not going to fight with a cripple."

"You won't even know there was a fight until you try to pull your head out of your ass."

The Senator's strong point was words, not physical action. "Easy, man. I just don't like strangers coming up here and making disparaging remarks about our meeting place."

"You call this rat hole a meeting place? What the hell kind of meetings are you talking about?"

"None of your damned business what our meetings are about. They're important."

Mary and another girl came in from the stairway. "Who's the straight arrow, Les? A cop?"

"He's my brother. Jeff, meet Mary and Bianca. They're part of the Thirteen."

Mary walked over and took Jeff's arm and rubbed her breasts against it. "Are you going to join us, brother Jeff?"

"Join you for what? I was just asking that sack of bones on the sofa what was going on here when you came in."

Mary gave Jeff a big smile and kept close to him. She had always thought that the Senator needed a good swift kick. Looks like someone might do it. "We're going to take over the world someday." she purred. "Would you like to be president?"

Les had dragged a big jug of cheap, red wine from a cupboard and poured out several glasses. He offered one to Jeff and indicated a chair for him to sit in. Jeff worked himself free from Mary and sat down. She noticed his missing foot for the first time "Holy shit. You've got no foot."

"I left it in Viet Nam. Long story."

"You're one of those goddamn baby killers?"

Les started to protest again, but Jeff stopped him. He hadn't liked the atmosphere of the place since he came in and he didn't want any more of it. He drained his wine glass and started to get up to leave. Les put his hand on Jeff's shoulder and held him in the chair. "No one calls my brother a baby killer. Who the hell do you people think you are. I brought him here to meet you because I thought you were my friends. I expected the Senator to be an asshole, but not the rest of you."

Bianca spoke for the first time. "If he's been in Viet Nam, he's not one of us. He's the enemy. Mary's right, and if you don't like it then fuck off."

Jeff and his buddies in Viet Nam had spent many an hour shooting the bull about the hippies and the war protesters and all the people back home that were bad mouthing the troops. Many of the guys in Nam had never actually met any of them. They went from high school to war without detours, or they came from small towns where more traditional values held sway. Maybe it was time to see what made these nuts tick. "Any more wine, Les? I need to get to know these buddies of yours." He leaned back in the chair and smiled at Mary and Bianca. Two more of the group had wandered in while Bianca was talking. Les didn't even bother to introduce them. "Let's sit down and talk, folks. I'd like to hear what you think the world is all about. Senator, what's your view of the real world?"

The Senator got up and walked over to Jeff. "I know the real world, soldier. It's right here. Not over in some fucking Chinese pagoda on the other side of the planet. Tough shit you got your foot shot off. That's what you get for going along with all those crap merchants in Washington."

"I'm going to tell you one last time, I'm a marine. And if you don't sit down and act nice you're going to find out what a pissed off marine looks like up close."

"Sure. That's your answer to the world's problems. Beat the crap out of anyone who doesn't agree with you."

"I didn't come in here with a chip on my shoulder. I came to meet some of my brother's friends, but you're such an irritating prick . . ."

"Okay, you want to talk, let's talk. What do you think the real world is all about? Is it the war mongers in D.C. that sent you and half a million of your killer buddies over to Viet Nam? Is the real world napalm and bombs? Is it dead babies?"

"The real world is the whole world. It's the good and the bad. I saw a lot of good in Viet Nam. Medics helping families with medicine. Engineers working on sanitation projects so there wouldn't be crap in the drinking water. I see good people in my home town. There's a hell of a lot more going on in the real world than war. All I hear you talk about is death and destruction. Don't you ever see anything else?"

"I haven't got time to sit around and watch the flowers grow. My job is to change the system. Our country isn't working right."

You may not be satisfied with the way things are going, but we have a way to deal with that. It's called voting. Ever done that?"

"Why the hell would I vote? There are no choices. Every one of those politicians is the same. Looking out for themselves and their rich friends."

"Then why don't you put up your own candidate, or better yet, run for public office yourself? Got the guts for that, Senator?"

Mary glared at Jeff. "Then he'd be one of them. We do better working from the outside."

"That's bullshit and a cop out. I learned something in Viet Nam. I am the government. If I don't take responsibility for making this country run right, then I'm the problem. I don't know if that war is right or wrong. Wasn't my place to decide. I joined the marines because I thought that was right. If the people running our government made a mistake in sending me over there, then that's the way it is. If it was wrong then it's my place to see that it doesn't happen again.

"Big fucking hero."

"There's always the possibility that it was the right thing to do. If that's the case, then maybe I was a hero. At least I tried to serve my country. What the hell are you goof balls doing?"

The Senator was beside himself. No one had ever come into this room and questioned what they were doing. "We're going to be the heroes when this is all over. Joining the marines or getting drafted is stupid. That war has nothing to do with us and no one from this country should be over there killing babies, or anyone else for that matter."

The Senator was losing his cool. Les' big brother wasn't as easy to intimidate as the rest of his cronies and he didn't know how to handle him. The other people in the room were more interested in the wine bottle than the revolution so they were less and less helpful in the argument. Jeff decided to bore in and see just how badly he could upset the Senator. "I think you're a goddamn coward. All this crap about the government and the politicians doing you wrong. You're just scared to death they may call your number. You don't have to worry. A chicken shit like you wouldn't last a day in boot camp."

"You can bet your ass I wouldn't. They'd never get me in one of those places. I refuse to enlist and I refuse to be drafted. It's not my war."

"How do you know which war is yours? It's your country. You take all the good, but when it's your turn to produce, you chicken out."

"I decide when to put my ass on the line."

"You haven't got the brains to decide. When they start letting snot heads like you make decisions, we're all in trouble. Les, how did you get yourself into this chicken coop?"

The Senator got off the sofa and moved in what he thought was a menacing fashion toward Jeff. He'd show this one-legged bastard he was no coward. He was about four feet away when Jeff sprang up on his good leg and rammed his crutch into the Senator's solar plexus. The skinny fellow doubled over and fell to the floor gasping for breath. Jeff grabbed his brother by the scruff of the neck and pushed him toward the door. Then he bowed gracefully to Mary and

Bianca. "I hope you yahoos get yourselves straightened out before it's too late."

Mary ran over to help the Senator. Bianca screamed at Jeff to get out and never come back. One of the guys that Jeff hadn't met got out of his chair and started toward Jeff, but he backed off when Jeff pointed one of his crutches right at the fellow's eye and calmly told him to sit down.

Jeff swung himself easily to the door and down the stairs thinking that the crutches made a pretty good weapon. Maybe he would keep them and forget the fake foot.

After leaving the infamous group of thirteen that his brother was involved with, Jeff realized that this world was a far different place than where he had spent the last year. Some of the comments he had just heard gave him pause to think. The frank appraisal of him losing his leg for a cause that was so terribly unpopular with so many people his own age jarred him a bit. He had grown up fast in the jungles of Viet Nam and had matured far beyond his years after meeting Nurse Jameson in the hospital in Da Nang. When he and Les got home he sat down and wrote her a long letter telling her how he felt, how things were different here in the States, and how he wished he could be with her. He went to bed and slept the peaceful sleep of the innocent dreaming of his beloved nurse, making plans to see her when she returned home. Even the thought of marriage didn't seem alien to him. In his letter he gave her both of his addresses, the one at the hospital and the one at his home. He wanted to hear from her and he didn't trust the postal service to get her letter to him. In fact, he suggested that she write to both places just to be sure.

The next morning the Dunlay family gathered around the breakfast table for the first time in many, many months. Anita was brighter and happier than anyone had seen her in recent weeks. Phil had a bit of a hangover, but he assumed his place as head of the household. The atmosphere was relaxed, almost normal. The conversation avoided the war and what it had done to them. There was talk about the garden, and getting the front porch painted, and cleaning out the garage. Jeff asked his dad for some advice on buying a car. Les mentioned his plans for going to college. Suzie wondered if she was ever going to find a boy friend. Amazingly, considering past events, the whole weekend remained pleasant. Jeff visited some high school buddies and rode around town with Les, but he spent Saturday evening at home with the family. On Sunday, Les was supposed to take Jeff back to the hospital, but Phil insisted that the whole family hop in the car and take the drive. When Jeff returned to his ward he had to regroup his thinking. He had almost forgotten where his life had led him over the past year.

Nurse Jamison had done exactly as Jeff had suggested. She sent a reply to his home and a copy to the hospital. It was a chatty, newsy letter with all kinds of information about the hospital where they had first met.

She told him to watch the newspapers and the magazines for a big story about a South Vietnamese soldier who was brought into the hospital with a live mortar shell in his side. It had gone in his shoulder, plowed along his rib cage and came to rest near his hip. It was a one in a million incident that it didn't explode. The doctors had the area around the operating table sandbagged and they brought in an explosive expert to disarm the thing after the doctor removed it. In the end they removed the shell and got it clear of the hospital without anyone being hurt. Nurse Jamison had cared for the soldier while he was being prepared for surgery. "Jeff, if that mortar had gone off, I'd be dead now," she wrote. "My guardian angel is watching out for me. I know that I'm going to get out of here alive, but between that incident and the rocket attack on the hospital last week, I've had cause to wonder."

She didn't come right out and say how she felt, but she did say that she missed him and was looking forward to seeing him when she got back to the world. Two more months and she would be on the big bird. No new duty assignment, but the Oakland Naval Hospital wasn't out of the question. If Jeff wasn't in too much of a hurry she could be his nurse again. First she had to go down to Saigon. There was a symposium for nurses in her category on new techniques, patient handling procedures, and better ways to help the wounded. She told Jeff that when she got back from Saigon she would have only forty-six days to go before she saw him again.

She kept the reunion part light and friendly. They could meet for lunch or dinner or something. However, the letter was signed "Love, Helen." That was the part that Jeff clung to.

CHAPTER 19

The routine at the hospital was boring and Jeff spent most of his days mooning over Nurse Jamison. He hadn't been back home since the episode with the "Thirteen" and the family get-together. It wasn't that there was a problem; he just wanted to get on with his therapy, get his new foot strapped on, and get all this hospital life behind him.

Another week went by before there was a letter with the Da Nang hospital for a return address. It was from a nurse, but not his nurse. It was from her roommate, the only other person who knew about the romance between the two. She opened her letter by saying how sorry she was that she was the one to tell the bad news. Nurse Jamison missed the regular flight back with the other nurses and had to hop a flight on a C-47 heading for Da Nang. As usual, the old gooney bird was loaded with ammunition, spare parts, people, and lord knows what other cargo. In fact it was overloaded. The plane was half way up the coast near Cam Rahn Bay when the pilot radioed that he had an emergency and would be coming in to land immediately. He was about three miles from the field when the left wing ripped off from the strain of being overloaded one too many times. There were no survivors among the debris in the South China Sea near the beach at Cam Rahn Bay.

Jeff woke up in a small room with his hands and legs tied to the bed. He felt like he had been beat up and drugged. That wasn't a bad description of what had happened to him. On his chart were the letters PTSD - post traumatic stress disorder. After Jeff had read the letter with the news of Nurse Jamison's death, he sat on the edge of his bed for a long time. All of the emotion that he had contained so capably and had dealt with since he came home erupted from his throat in a loud scream. He stood on his good leg and smashed his crutches over the bed. Then he turned the bed upside down. When the attendants got to him he was throwing bed pans, and glasses, and anything he could get his hands on all over the ward. He was raging and raving and screaming. Two attendants, some nurses and several of the other patients on the ward teamed up to subdue Jeff. A doctor administered a sedative and the torment was stifled.

Two days passed. The doctors gradually reduced the sedatives and allowed Jeff to come back to consciousness. The attendant on rounds saw that he was coming around and notified the psychiatrist. About two hours later the doctor finally made it down to the small room. "Kind of let it all go at once, eh, young fellow?"

"What's going on? Where am I."

"You're in an isolation wing Geoffery. You threw a bit of a wing-ding back on the ward. They snooped around after they calmed you down and found the letter that probably set this off. I'm sorry to hear about your friend."

From that moment on Jeff had two levels of recuperation and therapy to deal with, his body and his mind.

CHAPTER 20

When Jack returned to the States his orders read to take 30 days leave and return to his duties in Viet Nam. For the first two weeks at home he didn't think about going back. He had managed to put the navy world out of his mind. No duties, no uniforms, no LCDR Hilgo. His life centered on Sally and Todd and the fact that another baby was soon to arrive. He was content in the world of diapers, baby games and bedtime stories. It couldn't last. He could only block out the reality of his career for a while. He chose a time when Sally was out shopping to call his detail officer in Washington to ask what was being planned for him when his tour was over.

"Glad you called, Jack." Detail officers are born salesmen. They work on a first name basis and always give the impression that they have your best interests at heart. "I've been reviewing your record. You're going to be up for selection to Lieutenant Commander before you know it. You're on a fast track all the way except that R for Reserve behind your name. You have got to augment to regular navy now or all your good work is going to get lost. I have no doubt you'll be picked up as soon as your request hits the Bureau."

"I'm not so sure I want to stay in, Brian." Jack wasn't sure the silence on the other end of the line was because of what he had just said or because the first name familiarity only rolled downhill with rank.

"What the hell are you talking about? I just gave you the magic words -- 'Fast track' -- you're on your way up in the world of blue suits and gold stripes. Wide gold stripes, like admirals wear."

"Those are kind words and I'm sure you have the inside scoop, but I've had reason to rethink things and I'm not sure the navy is in my future."

"Would it make a difference if I offered you a plum assignment, shore duty, home every night, starting right now?"

"I still have three months to do back in Nam."

"I can justify cutting your tour to time served to date. Waste of government money to send you back over there for such a short time. How does an NROTC staff billet at the University of Washington sound to you?"

"You can do that?"

"I have the magic pencil, Jack. You tell me that your request for augmentation to regular navy is in the works and I start writing orders. Have your request in to the Bureau within ten days, with a copy on my desk, and you can cancel your flight to Saigon, pack up the family and go north."

Jack was stunned. The thought of going back to Viet Nam had become more of a problem than he could deal with. Being a prisoner had torn a hole in his shield of confidence. He wanted to hold his wife near him and never leave. What he feared most was that he was afraid to go back. How could he explain that to anyone. Facing fear and conquering it was what this business was all about. And it had to be done alone. If he went to the shrink and told him what he had been thinking, his career would be over; at least that's how Jack saw it. Now he was being offered an escape and no one would know. "Can I call you back? I have to run this by my wife and give it some thought."

"I need to start moving pretty quick on this, Jack. How soon can you get back to me?"

"I'll call you tomorrow, the next day at the latest."

When Sally got home about an hour later, Jack was sitting on the sofa where he was when he called his detail officer. "Oh, dear God, there's that two thousand yard stare again." When Jack didn't respond, Sally went over and sat next to him. "Anything wrong? Are you O.K., Jack?"

"I've just had some good news, honey."

"That's nice to hear. I can't imagine what condition you'd be in if you had bad news for me. What's going on?"

"I just got off the phone with my detail officer and he offered me an NROTC job up in Washington at the university."

"Is that the good news?"

"You sure know the system, don't you? Yeah, that's the good news. The bad news is that I have to go regular navy and settle in for the long haul to get the job."

"What about Viet Nam?"

"If I take this, it's over. We go directly to Washington. No more Nam."

Sally knew that there was more to this story than she was being told. It was a big decision, but not one that could create the agony she saw in Jack's eyes. "So you go regular, sign up for a few more years, and we get to play house for the next thirty-six months -- or is it a two year tour? Sounds pretty good to me. What's the real bad news?"

"If I don't go back to Viet Nam and face what's there, I'll never know if . . ."

"If what, if you can go to hell twice and come back? What is it, Jack? Are you afraid of something?"

"I'm afraid to go back. Afraid I'll die. Afraid I'll get captured again. Afraid I'll disgrace myself and everyone connected with me. I don't want to go back, but I have to. I have to know that I wasn't a coward."

"Dear God in heaven. Listen to yourself. You volunteered. You went where the bullets were. You faced being a prisoner. You have nothing to prove to anyone. Even the hot shots in Washington are telling you that you don't have to go back."

"No one else can answer this one. I have to figure out my own answer."

"I know someone who can help."

"No doctors, Sally. I don't want to talk to a doctor."

"I'm not thinking about a doctor. You need to talk to Jeff. You two know how each other feel better than anyone. Let me call Suzie and get his number at the hospital."

"How come I couldn't figure that out? You stay close to me, lady. I don't think so good on my own."

Sally got the number from Suzie and Jack called the naval hospital the next morning. He couldn't get through to Jeff, but when the volunteer on the phone heard who Jack was and his relationship to Jeff, he put him through to the psychiactric staff. It took a while, but Jack eventually got through to the doctor who was attending to Jeff. He agreed that Jack might be some good medicine right now. He wasn't aware of Jack's problem, but that didn't really matter. Jack said he would leave right away.

He arrived at the hospital shortly after noon. The hospital was a sprawling mass of buildings, some old some new. Jack wandered around for fifteen minutes following the directions of first one person, then another. All the while he was getting more and more anxious. If Jeff was in the looney ward this meeting might do more harm than good. What if the doctor started asking Jack questions. They might lock him up too. Fortunately he stumbled into the office he was looking for before he could back out. The doctor had alerted a corpsman to be on the lookout for Jack. He was escorted to Jeff's ward immediately.

Jeff was back in the regular ward. He was sitting in a wheel chair when Jack came in and he rolled over to him. "Let's go out in the back yard. I could use some sunshine."

Jack was a bit startled. He had expected Jeff to be in a padded cell. "Are you sure it's o.k?"

Jeff started to laugh. "No problem, Lieutenant. They gave me an anti-escape pill this morning."

"I'm sorry. When I talked to the doctor this morning, he said that you were having some problems. I just thought. . ."

Jeff waved his arm in front of him, sort of a time out signal. "I am having some problems, but not what you think. Before I left Viet Nam, I met a nurse. We had something going. She was due back in a few weeks. Word came that she didn't make it. Plane crash. Just like that it was all over. One minute I was in love and the next I had a piece of paper that said she was dead. When the news came, I went a little haywire. Hell, I went bugshit crazy. That's over now. I got a lot of crap out of my system in one big blowout."

"Sorry, didn't know about the nurse. You sure covered a lot of territory since I first met you."

"I'm being taken care of. Pretty much getting mind and body back in one piece. What brings you up here?"

"My wife sent me."

"That was nice of her. Any particular reason, or are you doing your good deed visiting broken down war veterans?"

"Actually, I need your help."

"Name it, Lieutenant. Anything I can do."

"I need to talk to someone. Things are kind of screwed up in my head. I was told today that I don't have to go back to Nam if I put in my papers to go regular and take a job up in Washington with the NROTC unit there."

"Sounds good to me. What's the problem?"

"This has to be between us, Jeff. And if you don't want to deal with it, just tell me."

Jeff had no idea what to expect. He wasn't used to having officers come to him for advice. This had to be a personal thing. "I'll help any way I can, sir."

"The first thing you can do is knock off the 'sir' crap. I'm here because right now you're the best friend I have. I owe you my life. The name is Jack."

"That cuts two ways, Jack. You don't owe me anything. We were in that mess together. We did what we had to do. I got lucky, that's all."

"What if I told you I was afraid to go back?"

"I'd say that you're pretty smart for an officer. You learned something while you were there."

"No joke, Jeff. I've got a knot the size of a basketball in my stomach. I have finally realized how close I came to dying. I'm afraid I will die if I go back. I'm afraid of being a coward."

Jeff looked down at the empty pant leg where his ankle and foot used to be, then he looked Jack square in the eye. "You talk to any man in this hospital and he'll tell you he feels the same way. I've had a few sessions with the shrink and we touched on this business. I know I'm not going back, but every once in a while I get that same knot. I get scared and I'm not even sure what I'm scared of. But I'm not ashamed of anything I did, and neither should you be. You did your job. You faced up to the worst they had to offer. I saw you when the chips were down. One thing, you're sure as hell no coward."

Jack returned Jeff's steady gaze. "What you say sounds good. And I guess you're right. But I feel like I'm bugging out. Someone has to do my job for me if I don't go back."

"Someone's doing your job right now. They can get along without you. What does your wife say about all this?"

"I told you. She sent me to see you. Said we've been there together and you would know how I felt."

"I'm not a doctor, Jack, but it sounds to me like you have some shit of your own to deal with. I think you should talk to one of these nut doctors; they're good. I had no idea how much shit I had stored up inside of me until I blew my cork. They brought me around, helped me see the problem. Lucky for me it came sooner than later. They tell me some guys go on for years getting more and more screwed up as they go along. The Big 3-D they call it. Drinking, drugs, divorce. You could be headed down that road."

"I can't tell anyone. My career would end at the doctor's office. I know these people."

"It's your decision. Our circumstances aren't anything alike. I don't have a career to worry about right now, but when I do, I don't want a six hundred pound gorilla on my back."

They talked for some time covering the same ground over and over. But Jeff couldn't convince his friend. "Thanks for your time, Jeff. You said all the right things. Better than any shrink could do. They can take Viet Nam and stuff it. I'm going to Washington. If things get rocky down the line there is still time to take your advice. For now, I'm going to let my family be the medicine I need."

"Good luck, sir ... er, Jack."

There was an awkward silence as the two shook hands. Jack finally leaned over and gave Jeff a hug. "Like it or not, I owe you. I want you to promise to keep in touch. I'll write as soon as we get settled in Washington. Maybe you can drop up for a visit. Might even be a good place to go to school." He left quickly, waving as he went through the door to the hospital corridor.

Washington. Jeff mused to himself. Why not? Change of scenery. A new life. Could start college. Might even get a job helping out with the football team. Maybe I'll take him up on that visit.

★ ★ ★

Jack was buoyed by Jeff's words of encouragement. "When the chips were down...you were no coward." He had said something like that. And Sally didn't think he was a coward. Even his detail officer said he was a fast track officer heading up. If everyone thought he was such a great guy then it must be so.

Sally was all smiles when Jack bounded through the door and told her to start packing; they were traveling north. He called his detail officer and told him there would be an augmentation request in the mail as soon as he could get over to Treasure Island and get some administrative help. Three days at the most.

"Good decision, Jack. I'll put a hold on your current orders and cancel them as soon as I get your letter. We'll probably keep you at Treasure Island. That's where you're administratively assigned now anyway. Shouldn't be for long."

It was only fair to write to Hilgo and tell him of the decision. Shouldn't make much difference to him. His tour was just about up. There would have been a whole new crew at the squadron headquarters about the time Jack got back. No one would even miss him.

Jack poured himself a large scotch and water and settled back on the sofa to contemplate his actions. The liquor tasted good. The problems were easing up and the fears were fading away. The second drink tasted even better. The war was over.

Jack was on his fourth scotch and water when Sally came into the living room and found him at the desk. The waste can was filled with the efforts to start the letter to Hilgo. Sally had no idea what demons were raging in Jack's head. "Writing your augmentation request?" Jack didn't respond. He just kept tapping his pen on the paper in front of him. Sally repeated her question.

"How the hell can I ask for augmentation into the regular navy when I don't even have the guts to go out and do the job assigned to me. Here I am trying to write to my old boss and tell him that I don't need to come back. I'm going to a safe job. You guys do the dirty work for me"

The words were starting to slur and Sally could see that Jack had been at the bottle pretty heavily. "Ease up, sailor. You've had a few too many. Things aren't in focus. Why don't you take a nap?"

Jack stood up, knocking over the chair and spilling his drink. "I need to make a phone call. And if you must know, I need another drink. Give me some time alone here, Sally. Get out and leave me alone for a while."

"What the hell is going on. You came in the door less than an hour ago and said we were going to Washington. Everything was rosy. What in the name of Christ happened? What's wrong, Jack?"

"Nothing's wrong. Everything is honkey-dorey. I finally realized that too many people are trying to run my life. I'm back in control and I'm going to decide what's best. I'm going to call that fucking detail officer and tell him to shove his hot deals and augmentation and all that other bull shit."

"I don't understand. Did someone say something to you? Did Jeff say something?"

"Leave Jeff out of this. He's the only friend I've got in the world. He understands. I started to write to Hilgo and I couldn't do it. I couldn't tell him that I was too scared to come back and that I took the easy way out. I can't do that."

"Let me make some coffee. Talk to me. Promise you won't do anything until we talk about this."

Jack wasn't listening. He poured another drink and sprawled on the sofa sipping at the mellow liquid. By the time Sally got back with the coffee, Jack was sound asleep. She threw a blanket over him and drew the blinds. "What the hell is going on?" she asked herself.

Jack woke up and stumbled to bed. He woke up the next morning feeling pretty good in spite of the night before. Sally was already downstairs in the kitchen. He showered and shaved and made his way to the kitchen, a bit sheepish. "What do you do with a drunken sailor, early in the morning? Isn't that how the song goes?"

"Sit down and have some breakfast. Then you can tell me what in the name of Lord Almighty happened to you yesterday."

"I had a little relapse. Guilt I guess. I was trying to write to Hilgo and tell him that I wouldn't be coming back and I just got more and more tangled up. I couldn't put the words down on paper. Maybe it's for the better. I got it out of my system. I think I've worked through the problem. I'm going over to T.I. today to get my augmentation letter put together."

"Do you want me to come along?"

"I don't think so. No telling how long it will take. No sense you and Todd having to sit in some waiting room." The doubts were there in spite of the front Jack was trying to put up. He wasn't sure he could write the augmentation letter.

Sally wasn't sure either, but she wanted to help Jack work this out. "Take your time. We have a long, easy livin' shore tour coming up."

CHAPTER 21

The ride to Treasure Island was almost like a morning commute. The traffic was heavy on the freeway and it slowed down even more as Jack got closer to the tollbooth. He finally got to the booth, paid his quarter and moved quickly onto the Oakland Bay Bridge. Half way across the bridge he took the turn-off to Treasure Island. The guard at the gate waved him through and he turned into the drive leading to the Administration Building. It was a beautiful old structure that once housed the offices of the 1939 World Fair for which the island was built.

Jack found his way to the admin office and explained what he was there for.

The woman officer that he was referred to seemed a bit confused by his request. Irritated was a better word. Here was one more unexpected requirement in her busy day. But she found an empty desk and dug out the necessary instructions and manuals for Jack to review. She told him she didn't have time to do his work too, but to let her know when he had a rough draft and she would try to find the time to go over it with him.

It was near noon before Jack had his draft ready. By that time, Lt. Yokodo, the officer that had been helping him, had caught up with her morning duties and was in a better mood. "Any plans for lunch? Most of us go over to the Officer's Club."

"Sounds good to me. Is the bar open at noon?" Jack remembered how easy the scotch went down yesterday and thought that one or two would help pass the afternoon.

"It's an officer's club. The bar is always open. I might even teach you how to play liar's dice if you buy me a drink. By the way, the name is Maio. Sorry if I was a little short with you this morning. It's been a bad week."

"Don't mention it. I've been a bit out of sorts myself this week."

Jack rode over to the club with Maio. He learned quite a bit about her on the short ride. She was of Japanese descent. Her husband was Officer in Charge of the Marine Detachment on the base. He was about to retire and she was leaving the service later in the year. They owned a small Japanese restaurant in San Francisco and planned to expand to bigger things when they got out.

Maio's husband Tim was waiting for her at the entrance. She gave him a peck on the cheek and a pinch on the ass in greeting. "Honey, meet Lt. Jack Walker, my administrative problem for the day. I told him that I would teach him how to play liar's dice."

The two men shook hands and eyed each other's ribbons, a quick review of one's military history. Tim had covered a lot of ground. World War II, Pacific Campaign, one battle star; Korea, four battle stars; Viet Nam, three stars. At the top of the rows of ribbons were a bronze star and a purple heart with one star, and finally a pair of paratrooper wings. Jack's display was adequate, but not as impressive as Tim's. He broke the ice. "Maio tells me you're about to hang it up."

"This is my last tour. Nicest thing the Corps has ever done for me. Put me near my wife. Easy living. About an hour's worth of paper work during the day and home every night. How about you? You going to be stationed here?"

Jack explained his plans over a martini. The three new friends rolled dice, talked, and got to know each other. They had a few more drinks and before Jack could protest, they were making plans to go over to the City for dinner. It was going to take the rest of the afternoon to get Jack's letter completed and checked over. Then

Miao had to get the Commanding Officer's endorsement. It was a simple formality. One word, "Forwarded." As Jack's administrative commander he would pass the request on to the Bureau. But this guy treated everything that came across his desk with suspicion. He would read Jack's letter, question every sentence, check the spelling, and want to know why he had to sign it. Miao knew the routine and was sure that she couldn't get a signature until tomorrow. She suggested that Jack get a room at the BOQ. He could enjoy a night on the town and check on his letter in the morning to be sure it got in the mail.

The idea appealed to Jack. He called Sally and told her the plan. She could tell that he had been drinking and asked him about it. "Just a cocktail before lunch. The Admin Officer and her husband insisted. They're the ones who are taking me to dinner. I'll be back in the BOQ before lights out. Should be home by noon tomorrow."

Sally had been right. Jack exchanged a few war stories with Tim and with the alcohol loosening him up he forgot all about ever thinking about getting out of the navy. Even the fears of going back to Viet Nam were gone. He was back on track, back in the military life.

After lunch, Jack worked on finishing his letter. Miao and her Chief Yeomen checked it over and got it typed. Jack hesitated for a moment before signing above his name. "Yes, this is what I want to do. 'Admiral Jack Walker.' Has a nice ring to it." He signed the letter and gave it to the yeoman for the endorsement. It was out of his hands and on the way to Washington, D.C.

It was about an hour before quitting time when he signed the letter. Jack told Miao that he had to go over to the Exchange and buy a toothbrush and some essentials if he was going to spend the night. He warned her that he had no civilian clothes and that she and Tim were going to have to put up with him in uniform at dinner. "No problem. We'll all go in uniform. Meet us at the club at 1630."

They had a drink at the club and decided on an early dinner. Tim had a personnel inspection planned for first thing in the morning. He wanted to get to bed at a reasonable hour. He suggested the Black Panther Steak House. "Don't let the name throw you. They have the best steaks in town." When they got there, Jack agreed. Soft lighting, live piano music, high backed booths, and the food was terrific. Jack made a note to plan an evening here with Sally as soon as possible.

It was a very pleasant evening, but unfortunately it ended too soon. Tim and Miao said their goodbyes at the front door. "Can you find your way back to the bridge okay?"

"No problem", said Jack "I'm an old San Francisco hand from way back. See you in the morning." He got to his car and started to head for the bridge, but as he was passing through North Beach he decided to stop for a drink. It was still early. Only eight o'clock. No sense moping around the BOQ all alone. There was a parking spot right in front of the Pink Owl. Good a place as any. Things hadn't started to warm up in the area yet. The neon signs were on and the music was blaring out of all the strip joints on the street, but there weren't many customers. Jack knew it wasn't a good idea to be down here in uniform, but he didn't plan to stay for more than one drink. He no sooner made it through the front door of the Pink Owl than a slightly overweight hostess in a skin tight black dress grabbed his hat off of his head and dragged him to a corner table. "Easy lady. I just want a quick drink."

"No problem, Admiral. Any reason you can't be a nice guy and buy me a drink too?" Jack started to protest but the woman pushed him into a chair before he could walk away. " What you drinking, Admiral?"

"Make it scotch, easy on the water."

The hostess signaled the bartender and hollered out the order. She was drinking a champagne cocktail. She moved her chair closer to Jack's and put her hand high on his thigh. "Tell me what you're doing here, Admiral. You're not checking up on us, are you."

"I'm just having a drink, lady. And stop calling me admiral." He took her hand and moved it off of his leg. She reached back over and gave him a little squeeze and he grabbed her hand more forcefully and pushed it away.

The hostess yelled out in mock pain. "Ouch! What the hell you doing, sailor? Don't get rough with me."

At that moment the bartender arrived with the drinks. "No rough stuff here, fella. You can't hold your booze, get the hell out. First you owe ten bucks for the drinks."

"Ten bucks? Fuck you. Drink it yourself." Jack started to get up to leave, but the hostess had moved around the table with his hat. When Jack tried to grab it, the bartender spun him around and pushed him back into his chair.

The bartender had hold of Jack's lapel and he had one knee on his stomach. "Ten bucks, asshole, or I take it out of your face."

Jack went into a rage. He brought the heel of his hand up under the bartender's chin hard enough to move him backwards. Then he came out of the chair and kneed him in the groin and as the bigger man doubled over in pain, Jack brought his knee up into his face as he pushed his head down. The man crumbled to the floor. The hostess started to scream and Jack reached over, grabbed his hat and swatted her with it. He took his drink and downed it in one gulp. Then he took a five-dollar bill out of his wallet and threw it on the table. He looked around the bar. There were only two other people in the place and they hardly paid any attention to the fracas in the corner. Best thing to do was to get the hell out of here, thought Jack. Back out on the street he started to feel a bit nervous. What if the bartender came after him with a gun or something? He found himself walking quickly down the street and around the corner. No one was following him. He almost bumped into the hustler out in front of The Olive, another noisy joint.

"Come on in and have a drink, buddy. No cover charge until nine o'clock. Give this token to the bartender and the first drink is a double. Step right inside." The hustler had Jack through the door even more smoothly than the hostess in the last place had maneuvered him.

Jack ordered scotch on the rocks. "Your friend outside said you'd make it a double for this token." He flipped the little coin to the man behind the bar.

"He told you right, pal. I'll make 'em both doubles."

"I just want one drink, not two."

"House rule. Two drink minimum. What the hell's the difference, you're going to have a couple anyway, right? Ten bucks. Drink up."

"When in Rome" thought Jack. He pulled a ten from his wallet and dropped it on the bar. He downed the first drink before he realized that it was lousy scotch. Then he settled onto the bar stool and started nursing the second drink. After awhile, he realized that he was going to get too drunk to drive back to the base if he didn't quit now. He pulled a couple of ones from his pocket and tucked them under his glass as a tip and pushed them across the bar. Before he could get off the stool, the bartender was there with a new drink. He swept up the dollar bills along with the empty glass and told Jack it was on the house.

Just then the band struck up and a well-shaped blonde danced out onto a small stage across from the bar. "What the hell" thought Jack,

"One more for the road." He finished the drink quickly and headed for the men's room. He knew that he had to leave and get back to the base. His plan was to keep on walking past the bar when he left the toilet and get back to his car before someone else cornered him. In his mind he was making a bigger plan than was necessary. The drinks had gotten to him. He was drunk, but functioning. But he went through with the plan and made it back to the sidewalk. The hustler tried to steer him back into the bar, but Jack resisted and kept walking. About the time he got to his car he realized that he didn't have his hat. "Oh, shit. I've got to get my hat. Might as well be bare-assed as bare-headed in this man's navy."

As he turned to go back he lost his balance and fell against the fender of his car and into the gutter, right into a puddle. He got up and tried to brush the water and dirt off of his uniform but ended up making more of a mess. "Forget the hat. I've got to get the hell out of here."

Then his luck turned bad. The hostess from the Pink Owl had stepped out of the bar for a breath of air and had seen Jack coming up the street. She ran in and told the bartender. He went right to the phone and made a quick call, and then he went to the front door. In less than a minute after the call a police car pulled up out in front.

"That's him, officer. Hit me, hit the hostess, and took off without paying his tab."

Jack was fumbling with his car key when the two cops grabbed his arms and handcuffed him. "You come with us, tough guy. We'll give you a ride." They dumped him in the back of the patrol car and waived to the bartender. "Tell your boss not to forget our envelope come the first of the month."

The two cops debated in loud voices whether to take Jack to the station house, or just kick the shit out of him and dump him in an alley. "Take me to the shore patrol. I'm in the navy." One of the cops leaned over the back seat and Jack thought he was going to hit him, but the cop just laughed.

"You're one sorry assed looking navy man. I was a marine. Never saw a marine officer screwed up like you."

"Give me a break. I just got back from Nam. I'm not used to the booze. I overdid it. Why did you pick me up? I didn't do anything except fall down."

"How about beating up that bartender and the hostess and then skipping out on your bar tab? Call that nothing?"

"That son of a bitch hit me first. And the goddamned hostess tried to steal my hat. And I paid for the fucking drink. Is that why you picked me up? Because that bartender told you to?"

The patrol car pulled up in front of a nondescript building and one of the cops got out and opened Jack's door. Jack was terrified. He thought they were going to kill him. The cop pulled him out of the back seat and he fell to the pavement. He was pulled to his feet and hustled through the half open door of the old building. He was about to plead for his life when he saw the navy petty officer with a shore patrol brassard on his arm seated at a desk in front of him. The cop took off the handcuffs and told the petty officer that he had one fucked-up navy officer here and that if they didn't keep him off the streets he was heading for the drunk tank.

"We'll take care of him." The petty officer motioned to another sailor to take Jack over to a bench and have him sit down.

Jack asked, "What are you going to do? Can I leave?"

"Sorry, Lieutenant. My orders are to move you to the brig at T.I. as soon as possible. You'll probably get to talk to the Commandant himself tomorrow."

The liquor was taking its full effect and Jack was less and less able to understand what was happening to him. He started to doze off. He was only half awake when the shore patrol loaded him into the van for the trip to Treasure Island.

Jack woke up about four in the morning. He was in a cell with two other people. They were on bunks and he was on the floor. Slowly the realization of what had happened to him came clear. He was in big trouble. Fortunately there was a commode in the cell. Jack threw up a goodly amount of bad scotch. He rinsed his face in the basin and dried his hands and face on his shirt. His uniform jacket was lying in a heap in the corner. He went over and picked it up. It was a mess. His trousers were filthy. He needed a shower and a shave and a change of clothes. But none of those things were available. He was just another bum in a drunk tank, and up to his ass in bad times. He found his empty bunk and crawled into it.

Jack didn't realize that he had slept for almost an hour when the marine guard came by banging his nightstick on the bars and yelling "Reveille, reveille, drop your cocks and grab your socks. Everybody up. Reveille."

Jack and his cellmates got up and stood facing the bars. Two guards carrying nightsticks unlocked the door and ordered them out into the passageway. One guard tapped the other two men on the chest with his nightstick, ordered them to attention, and marched them down the passageway. The other guard said, "Please come with me sir." and led Jack in the opposite direction. There were the usual catcalls from various cells as the officer was led by. The guard quickly silenced them. They went through two security doors and into a wider hall. The guard knocked on the door marked "Officer-in-Charge" and stood at attention waiting for orders to enter. Jack heard Tim's voice bellow out "Come in." The guard turned to Jack, opening the door at the same time. "Please step inside, sir."

The door closed behind him and Jack was standing at Tim's desk. The captain was in his dress uniform. His white gloves, sword, and hat were neatly arranged to one side of the desk. "Am I glad to see you, Tim."

"Save it, Lieutenant. You're not glad to see me and I sure as hell am not glad to see you. You will address me as Captain Harrigan. It is my duty to inform you that you are to report to the Commanding Officer of the Naval Station at zero eight hundred. You have been charged with drunkenness and conduct unbecoming an officer. The formal charges will be read at Captain's Mast."

Jack felt he was going to be sick again but he held on. The look of contempt on Tim's face added to the misery. "I can't go to Mast looking like this. Can I get cleaned up? I don't even have my hat."

"Normally, Lieutenant, you'd go just the way you are. You don't deserve any consideration after disgracing your uniform. But it seems that a certain officer in the admin department has a soft spot for you. Get your clothes off and put them on that chair. You can use my washroom to clean up. There's a razor on the shelf. I can't promise anything, but we'll try to press out your uniform. Get moving, we leave in thirty minutes for your Captain's Mast."

Twenty minutes later Jack was shaved and fairly well cleaned up. His uniform was a different story. There hadn't been time to do much except give it a fast sponging an a press. It only helped a little bit. His shirt was beyond help. Luckily Tim had a black tie to replace the one Jack had thrown up on. He was still a sorry looking sight, but somewhat better off than he was a half hour before.

"I'm sick, Tim. Any chance you have a bottle in here?"

"If I did, I'd hit you with it before I'd give you a drink. Shape up now, Lieutenant, and stop feeling sorry for yourself. That's what got you into this mess. I could see it last night at dinner. You think you've got a war-connected disability. You think the world owes you something because you got knocked around in Viet Nam." Without warning, Tim grabbed Jack by the lapel and slapped him hard across the face. Then he shoved him against the wall and held him at arms length. "You're a sorry assed fuck-up, Lieutenant. Twenty-four hours ago the world was treating you like a gold plated hero, and you fucked it up. If we weren't on the way to see the old man, I'd punch the shit out of you here and now."

When Tim released his grip Jack almost fell to the floor. "I need a drink. Just to get me through Mast."

"The only thing you get is out that door. I don't want to be seen with you, but my job this morning is to escort you personally. I hope he hangs your ass. Get moving."

They went out a side door to a waiting car. The Commanding Officer's office was only three blocks away, normally a short walk for Captain Tim Harrigan, but this morning he chose to ride rather than be seen escorting a disheveled naval officer that didn't even have a complete uniform in which to present himself. No one spoke during the brief ride.   On arrival, Tim got out of the car and indicated for Jack to follow him. Work stopped at most of the desks as the two marched past. To call the appearance of the two officers a contrast would be a decided understatement. They went up to the second floor where the captain held mast. There was a crowd of people in the hallway waiting for eight o'clock. The base commander was acting commanding officer for the hundreds of transient personnel passing through T.I. on orders from one base to another. Most of the cases up for Mast were sailors who overstayed their leave. Most turned themselves in well before the thirty- day desertion charge became effective. Simple AWOL. Absent Without Official Leave. A few were there for fighting or theft. The charges ranged from unimportant to very serious. Murder and rape were not frequent, but neither were they unheard of.

What was unusual was to find an officer at Mast. The threat of a bad notation on a fitness report was usually enough to keep most officers in line. They came from a background of discipline and ambition that usually gave them pause to think twice before committing acts of transgression, that and the fact that officer problems were normally handled off the record. Department heads and executive officers took unofficial action early on and impressed their will on those who strayed. Things rarely got to the Old Man.

But this was a different case. Jack was a fish out of water. He was just another transient. He had no established contacts. The people who had dealt with him the night before followed orders, no more, no less. Tim Harrigan could have helped him if someone had notified him that an officer was in custody, which might have been done if someone in the chain of events had known who Jack was. But that was not the case. He went to a cell and the official report went to the Base Commander. Once the report was filed, it could not be changed. To help someone, you had to do it before the paperwork began.

"Lieutenant John Walker, front and center." Jack braced himself and stepped before Captain Grossbock. He stood at attention, eyes straight ahead.

An officer read the summary. "Lieutenant Walker is reported to have become drunk and disorderly in a public place, fought with a civilian in a public bar, was out of uniform on a public street, and was attempting to get into his car in a drunken state when apprehended by civilian police in San Francisco." The charges were read in a dispassionate manner by the junior officer assigned to the command staff who then advised Jack that he did not have to make any statement, but that anything he did say could be used against him in the event of a court martial.

Captain Grossbock took over. "Lieutenant Walker, you have been advised that you do not have to make any statement; however, I have the authority at this level to discipline you myself, refer you to a court martial, or dismiss this incident entirely. I would like to hear your side of what brought you in front of me in such a deplorable condition. Where is your hat, Lieutenant?"

"I lost it, sir. I'm not sure where."

True to his nature, Captain Grossbock chose to dwell on the trivial at the expense of the more serious events at hand. "Bad enough you act disgracefully in a civilian environment, but I find it intolerable that you can't even come before me a complete uniform."

Jack was going to respond, but there was nothing to say. He could barely stand up straight and he knew that if he had to stand there much longer he was going to throw up. "I asked for this", he thought to himself. "Just like my old man, I'm a useless drunk."

"Well, are you going to tell me what brought you to this sorry state?" The captain was leaning forward over the lectern that he stood behind to conduct Mast. "What are you doing here anyway?"

He turned to the officer assisting him. "Why is this officer attached to my command?"

The young officer answered with the same dispassionate voice he used to read the charges. "He's on leave from his unit in Viet Nam. He is attached to us administratively for that period."

"Why are you on leave, Mister? The captain felt he was on to something that needed dealing with. "Why are you back here instead of at your post in Viet Nam?"

This was taking a turn that Jack hadn't expected. He glanced over at Tim Harrigan who maintained his look of disgust from earlier. What could he say that would make all this go away without sounding like he was whining. "I regret my actions of last night. I have no excuse. I am on leave because I was a prisoner of war for a short period after a boat I was on was sunk by rocket fire. I believe it is termed as recuperation leave. I came here yesterday to request administrative assistance in preparing a letter of request for regular navy augmentation. The letter should be on the captain's desk now."

Captain Grossbock stared at Jack in disbelief. "You expect me to consider you for regular navy augmentation after this incident. I have absolutely no intention..." Suddenly the captain stopped talking and drew back as Jack leaned over and grabbed a nearby waste basket. He retched violently into the bucket.

Tim Harrigan broke the embarrassed silence. "Sir, I suggest that Lt. Walker be taken to Sick Bay for a medical evaluation." He took a handkerchief from his pocket and handed it to Jack as he helped him to his feet. "This man is sick, sir."

"You bet he's sick. Get him out of here; and I want a medical report on my desk within the hour. I want to know when I can resume Mast on this officer. And someone find a hat for him to wear. He can't be running around my base out of uniform, sick or not."

Tim Harrigan felt a real compassion for Jack. He had thought earlier that shock treatment would help. That's why he had told him to shape up and stop feeling sorry for himself. But he knew enough about combat and its effects on men to see that Jack needed help. There was something in the way he had stated that he had been a prisoner, and there was a genuine pain in his eyes when he mentioned the rocket attack that sank his boat. If only he had stayed with Jack another hour or so last night. This whole mess could have been averted. He sent word for his assistant to conduct the scheduled marine barracks personnel inspection. He had decided to give Jack all the help he could.

The base dispensary was small by most hospital standards, but it was well staffed and equipped to handle medical emergencies and shortterm recoveries. In the car on the way over, Tim told Jack that he needed to get whatever was bothering him off his chest. He was in hot water, but the best thing to do now was to get out of the clutches of Captain Grossbock. "That guy will fuck you up like a Christmas Goose. Talk to the doc. Have them send you to Oak Knoll for an evaluation of the inside of your head. It's a sneaky way to go, but it's the only way to make all this bullshit go away."

"If I go to the shrink, my chances for regular navy are down the drain."

"Your chances for regular navy are back there in Grossbock's trash bucket along with all that cheap booze you barfed up. You've got one chance to get clear. You go back to Mast and you're facing a court martial. I'm not sure what the navy penalty is for losing your hat, but Grossbock is looking to hang your ass because you showed up without one this morning."

Tim had a brief conversation with the doctor before turning Jack over to him. The session in the doctor's office was short. It was the genesis of a grand conspiracy that would have been considered mutiny if it were not for the fact that everyone involved felt that God was on his side. All it took to get things started was for Tim Harrigan to tell the doctor that Grossbock was trying to railroad a good officer for going out on a toot. The opportunity to run the captain's train off the track was an incentive to every officer on the base.

Within thirty minutes of arriving at the dispensary Jack was on his way to Oak Knoll. The doctor's medical report went to Grossbock with the recommendation that Jack be transferred to the hospital immediately. Somehow, the augmentation letter to regular navy disappeared from Captain Grossbock's "in basket". And the folder containing the preliminary mast report and shore patrol write-up went astray.

Lt. Yokodo reported to Captain Grossbock that it looked as if that officer named Walker that was here for Mast this morning was on his way to a psychiatric discharge. Nothing she could confirm, but someone at the dispensary mentioned it when she had called on another matter earlier in the morning. "Sounds like the guy cracked up."

Captain Grossbock looked quite pleased. "I knew there was something wrong with that man. Can't fool me. I know people and that man was not officer material. It's a wonder he got as far as he did. Where is that augmentation letter of his? I want to endorse it 'disapproved'."

"He never gave it to us, sir. I think he spent the whole day at the bar. Never did get the letter written. Good riddance, I say."

CHAPTER 22

Sally met Jack in the outpatient waiting room at the hospital. She brought the fresh uniform he had asked for and she had Todd dressed up in his best sailor suit. "Does all this mean I should unpack my suitcase?"

"I don't think we'll be going to Washington just yet. I had a talk with Brian, my detailer, a few minutes ago. Told him what had happened. He said no harm done yet if I can get past the shrink. Turns out I wasn't going to get the billet anyway. The detailer's boss was pissed because he was cutting my tour short and making promises about the regular navy thing. Brian wasn't sure how I was going to take it and he was almost happy that I had screwed myself up."

"Does this mean that you are going back to Viet Nam?" Sally tired to make it sound like conversation, but her trembling lip gave her away.

"I'm not sure. If I go back to Treasure Island, the C.O. there is waiting to court martial me. If I stay here in the hospital, I'll end up with a medical discharge. I don't think I have any choice."

A corpsman at the desk called out Jack's name and told him where to find the doctor's office where his appointment was scheduled. Sally said that she and Todd would be in the cafeteria.

The session with the psychiatrist lasted just under an hour. "From what I can see, you ordered your own best prescription. A bit unorthodox; you may have gone overboard getting yourself arrested, but all-in-all you needed to blow off some steam. If I had my way, you wouldn't go back to Viet Nam right now. But if you stay in the navy, you are going to run into this problem again some day. And you're going to wonder if you're up to it. All natural reactions."

"Are you saying that I should go back?"

"From what you've told me, you don't have much choice. You're not crazy, so I'm not going to keep you here. You don't seem to be a danger to yourself or anyone around you, so I not going to recommend that you go to jail. You've faced a lot, Jack. More than most people. I think you can handle it; just stop trying to do it all on your own. Let your family and friends help you. That gang at T.I. saved your bacon this morning. You're a good officer. People see that and they will help you if you let them. Put this behind you and get on with your career. We'll hold your records here until you go back, if that's what you decide to do."

Jack walked down to the cafeteria. Sally and Todd were waiting. "What's the news, Jack? And this time you tell me what the hell is going on or I swear I'll divorce you before the coffee gets cold!"

Jack explained what the doctor had told him. Then he filled Sally in on what he could remember about the night before. It was hard to believe that all of this had taken place in just one day. He outlined his options as he saw them and leaned back in his chair to wait for Sally to digest all the information. He knew that once she sorted it all out that she would give him a straight from the shoulder recommendation. She had a way of going to the heart of a problem.

Her response threw him. "I can't answer this one for you, Jack. I think you've told me everything about how you feel, but there are things in your head that no one can know about." She took his two hands in hers and gave him a look that melted him. "I love you, Jack. And I know that you love me. This is a crisis in our lives, and you have to solve it. I'll do anything you ask. I'm putting my future and our kids' existence in your hands. Whatever you say is what we will all do."

Jack knew responsibility. He had made decisions that put men's lives in harm's way. He had faced death. But this was toughest position he had ever been in. He wasn't dealing with military people who were trained to give a cheery "aye aye, sir" and go on with the job. This was the woman he loved telling him to decide her fate.

"I guess I have thought about it, Sally. I knew what I was supposed to do from the beginning. At least about going back. We're going to have to talk about this navy career sometime. For now, we have to go over to San Francisco and pick up the car, and then we'll go home. My leave is up in a week and I don't want to waste any of it."

CHAPTER 23

"Sit down, Lieutenant. We need to have a little chat." Lieutenant Commander Hilgo hadn't lost any of his aristocratic, authoritative bearing, but there was a softening of the hard edge that Jack had seen earlier in their relationship.

"Thank you, sir."

"I'm surprised to see you back here, Jack. I would have thought that the Bureau could have found you a rewarding stateside billet after all you went through."

Jack wasn't sure how to respond. His mind raced back over the past few weeks, his trouble in San Francisco, his talk with the psychiatrist, his meeting with Jeff at the hospital. And then there was Sally's reply when he asked for help. "I'll do whatever you want, but you have to make this decision." He decided to follow the doctor's advice and give people a chance to help him. "I was this close to not coming back, Skipper."

Contrary to what Jack might have expected, Hilgo softened even more being called by the familiar term "Skipper". The mantle of command had brought out his human side. "What changed things?"

Jack opened up with all of his fears and frustrations. He told Hilgo about being afraid to come back. He explained the offer of the billet in Washington. He even told him about the night in the brig, and how a group of strangers saved his bacon. He told him everything.

Hilgo was quiet after Jack finished his story. He took off his glasses and laid them carefully in the middle of his desk. Then he leaned back in his chair and fixed his gaze directly into Jack's eyes. "Hell of a story, Jack. Now you're back here. Full circle. Can you handle it?"

"I don't know."

"I'm glad you told me what's eating at you. You've been through hell. I understand what you have to deal with. I'm going to make it easier for you and I don't want any arguments. You have less than three months to go on your tour. You will spend them at your desk. No more unauthorized rides on the boats. You have nothing to prove."

Jack started to protest immediately. "If I don't get out there at least once, I'll never know."

"Somehow I knew you would say something like that. So here's the deal. You get one ride. I pick the boat and the time. Agreed?"

"I know what you're doing, Commander, and I appreciate it. But I don't want any favors, I can't go home not knowing if I can hack it."

"You've already hacked it. Besides, your job is operations officer of this outfit. Parks is gone and there is no relief yet. Fixcue's replacement is green as grass, and I've got three new boat skippers to break in. I'm short handed and I need your help here at headquarters. You have to double as my X.O. until the new C.O. is ordered in. I'm ordering you to stay at your desk for my benefit, not yours."

Everything Hilgo had said was based on fact. Jack found that he was relieved at the way things were turning out. Maybe that shrink back at Oak Knoll knew what he was talking about after all.

As Jack stood to leave the office, Hilgo had one last word for him. "Just because I said you had to act as my X.O. doesn't mean that you move into my old office. I've got it set up the way I want it. When the new Commanding Officer arrives I'll be moving back in there, so use your old desk."

"Yes, sir," smiled Jack. It was comforting to have the old Hilgo back. The pace picked up almost immediately and the first month of Jack's tour went by in a blur. Hilgo had not been kidding; there was more going on than Jack could keep up with. And in addition to everything else, he had Sally to worry about.

The baby was due just about the time Jack had been scheduled to return to Viet Nam. He wanted to get an extension on his leave, but Sally was adamant. "You get on that goddamned plane and get that goddamned tour of duty over with. I'm not going to go through another two weeks like the last ones we just finished. Just go, and get it over with! I'll be fine."

For a short period, Jack felt he was going over the edge again. Sally was his whole life and she was going to have a baby, and he was going back to the war. Things couldn't be any worse. But in the end, Sally convinced him to do what he had to do. She sat him down and talked logic to him until he knew it was his duty to leave.

Eight days after Jack arrived back in Da Nang, the Red Cross notified him that he was the father of a seven pound, three ounce baby girl. Mother and daughter were doing fine. Sally had gotten a promise she wasn't expecting from the lady next door who had helped her before. She was told, "Don't worry about a thing. I have nothing to do for the next month but take care of Todd. When you get home from the hospital, I'll be here, and I'll take care of you, too."

There was also Susan Dunlay that Sally could call on if necessary. The two of them had become good friends and Susan was crazy about Todd. Things had changed so much in the last months. There were new friends willing to help, and that made a world of difference. Sally wasn't alone anymore. It was almost too good to be true, but Sally had learned a lesson too. If someone wants to help you, then for crying out loud, let her help.

When Jack finally realized that Sally was in good hands and that all was well on the home front, he settled down to the daily routine and got back in the groove. His duties as executive officer were not very demanding. Hilgo had a hard time letting go and he incorporated the job into his own as commanding officer.

Brick Swartz had extended his tour by six months and he made things even more normal for Jack. Because of the busy schedule, there were fewer of the evening beer sessions in Jack's room, but there was always a cold one waiting when the occasion arose. Hilgo had seen to it that the room was untouched while Jack was gone – even the refrigerator was waiting for him.

Whenever he had a spare moment, Jack tried to reach Karpaski. He wasn't at the unit he told Jack he was assigned to; he must have been reassigned somewhere in the process. Sally had been busy having a baby and didn't reach his wife before she moved back east. It was another one of those promises to keep in touch that would fall by the wayside. Jack finally gave up trying to reach him with the hope that they would meet again sometime. It reminded him of Buck, the Air Force officer in Saigon; one day he was a bosom buddy and the next day he was gone forever.

Every day, Jack promised himself that he would write down the names of the people he was working with and at least get them on a Christmas list. When he finally found himself boarding a plane at Tan Son Nuit to return home, he didn't have one address in his pocket.

Jack sat back in his seat on the plane and he thought over his last three months of duty; now that his tour was officially over, he was pleased with how things had turned out. He never did get his boat ride; there just hadn't been time. Hilgo was transferred a week after the new commanding officer reported, and his executive officer arrived a week later. Jack played a key part in the operation of the squadron in the beginning, but the new officers soon fell into the routine and the outfit started running better than it ever had. The time for Jack to leave had arrived.

Jack was still thinking about augmenting to regular navy as his tour wound down when a surprise arrived in the mail. He had been selected as a TAR officer. It was a special classification of officers assigned to a primary duty training naval reservists. If he chose to accept the designation then orders assigning him to duty as Commanding Officer of a Reserve Center in Seattle, Washington would follow. The TAR offer was a whole new wrinkle in the fabric and he didn't know what it was all about.

Two nights later, in the officer's club bar, Jack was having a drink with a commander who had recently arrived in Da Nang. They were just shooting the breeze when Jack mentioned the TAR billet. He was explaining his ignorance of the program when the commander offered to explain what it was all about. It turned out that he was a TAR. The only reason he was in Viet Nam was because he had volunteered. TARs usually stayed in their own circle between reserve centers, district staffs, and duty in either the Omaha Headquarters or Washington, D.C. An added benefit was that they competed within their own group for promotion so there was no problem with trying to match up with regular navy officers.

It didn't take Jack long to make his decision. He was heading for Seattle after all. He had made a quick phone call to Sally to explain the new idea and she gave it the highest stamp of approval. He had gotten the paperwork completed and his life started to feel pretty good. Now he was a few hours from home, and when he held Sally in his arms life would be glorious.

When the passengers were discharged from the plane at Travis Air Force Base, things were a bit quieter than the previous time Jack was there. Sally had promised not to speed or crash the main gate on her arrival, and except for her parking in a restricted zone, she was a model navy wife. Jack managed to get her back in the car and off the base before any trouble started.

Jack had his orders in his hands and he had 30 days to get to Seattle and his new billet. First, he made a point of a going to Treasure Island to look up Miao and Tim. He wanted them to know that their faith in him had been justified. This time Sally was with him when he arrived at the Admin office. Miao let out a whoop when she saw him and told him to take a seat and not to move. She ran to her office and returned shortly with a pile of papers. It was the TAR promotion list and Jack's name was listed with the new Lieutenant Commanders. Tim showed up a few minutes later and another reunion was underway. Jack suggested they meet at the Black Panther for dinner, his treat. This time, he had a chaperone so everyone could relax. The party ended early with all the usual promises to stay in touch, and the next day Jack and Sally were on the road north.

The drive to Seattle was like a second honeymoon. They took their time and enjoyed every minute on the road. When they arrived in Seattle, there was a letter waiting with a wonderful surprise. In the envelope were season tickets for the coming season's Washington Huskies football games -- complements of Jeff Dunlay, Team Manager.

Finis